Mine to Possess

Veteran K9 Team
Book 3

Kameron Claire

Snuggle Whore Press, LLC

Editor: Shay M Williams

Covers by SWP Covers

!! Formerly titled: Bunny Hill Betty !!

Dedication

This series is dedicated to every individual
who signs a blank check on their ass
by enlisting in the Armed Forces
to serve their country—and to the
loved ones who support them back home.

We are Witty, Wicked & Wild wherever we go!

VETERAN
K9
TEAM
REPORTING
FOR DUTY

Chapter One
Barron

"You ready?" I raise my brow as Linc walks in from his first training session with Nanook, a two-year-old Husky. The dog's owner, a PTSD counselor named Jamie, wants to use her fur demon as an emotional support animal well-behaved enough to take to the VA center.

Apparently, his first visit resulted in them being kicked out after he stole a cheeseburger from a patient.

Hence why we call him a demon, but we'll get him set right in no time.

"Yeah." Linc grabs his backpack from his chair. "I'm excited about this job, man. First day of the ski season."

"Technically, this is their soft opening. Thanksgiving is always the opening weekend, but we've had decent early snowfall, so here we go."

"I can't thank you enough for getting me this side hustle. I need the cash, and I can't think of anything better than this cush position."

"Is it cush?" I stand and grab my keys, knowing damn well it is a sweet gig. Payment, overnight lodging, and all the skiing we can fit in when we're not working—the job is cake. I grab my small go pack, my overnight bag and skis already in my truck along with Linc's.

He'll leave his car here for the weekend.

No reason for both of us to drive.

Karden walks into the office with a younger guy who still has that active duty military veneer to him. Clean shaven, tapered haircut, almost rigid posture. "Hey guys. This is Logan, but you might hear me slip up and call him Hollywood from time to time."

Linc drops his bag and offers the guy his hand. "Holy shit, man. What the fuck are you doing here?"

The young guy, who does have movie star good looks, smiles widely and shakes his hand. "I'm here to check out the facility."

"You're the investor?" Linc's jaw drops. "Goddamn. I guess the rumors were true."

Hollywood shrugs, but neither man elaborates for my curious mind.

There's been talk around the office that Janey found an investor for the center, one who could help us turn this place into the vision we have for the future. And when I say we, I mean all of us, because Janey promised when we signed on for peanuts that we'd all get stock in the company when the time came.

I guess that time is coming sooner than expected.

For someone like me with a full military retirement, the barely minimum wage we make here doesn't affect my living standards like it does Linc, who only did a little under eight years in the Army. While he is a disabled veteran like the rest of us, his monthly VA check isn't enough to keep him fat in cash. I think he has enough saved up from all the deployments to let him ride for a couple years, but if things don't change in that time, I don't know if he'll be able to stay on without finding a better paying job.

Hence why I got him the gig on the mountain. He ETS'd nine months after me and I knew he didn't want to go back to Arkansas anymore than I wanted to go back to Missouri.

Logan rubs his smooth jaw. "I thought you wanted to be a paratrooper, not K9."

Linc shakes his head. "That's a long story. One I don't have time to tell."

"Yeah, we've got to get up to the mountain and get clocked in," I interject and offer Logan my hand. "Barron Theroux."

"Sergeant Major Theroux? Damn, I've heard of you."

Before I can ask what that means, Linc hauls his backpack up on his shoulder and nods. "We work search and rescue at Silver Mountain Ski Resort two weekends a month. Occasionally we take on ski instruction, but only if the lodge bunny is super hot."

Hollywood snorts. "You haven't changed one bit."

"Hell, no. Why mess with perfection?" Linc flashes his cocky smile, the one that has gotten him into more trouble than out of.

I roll my eyes and make a move for the door with my

old German Shepherd, Sarge, following behind me. With her advanced age and arthritis, she no longer works, but stays by my side whenever possible. "We'll see you guys Monday."

I pass Kemp and Janey on the way to my truck, mock saluting them with two fingers without saying a word. Neither Kemp nor I are big talkers, and Janey is walking with intent, which I guess means she's rushing inside to meet with the investor.

Jesus. A mid-twenty-year-old investor?

I have to hear the backstory of this guy, because I don't know of any enlisted Army guys that can afford to buy a house, much less invest in a business like ours. Last I heard, Janey was looking for a couple million—a sum that none of us can come close to covering.

Linc meets me at my truck a few minutes later and settles his Husky Li-Lou in the back on her bed next to Sarge before plopping his ass into the passenger seat. Without speaking a word, I hit the northbound highway to skirt around Spring City, taking the back roads to merge onto I-70 east of the tunnels.

"So, what's the rumor?" I finally ask.

"Huh?" Linc looks up from the game on his phone. He's always got to be doing something, his old age chill still years away from settling into his bones. That's one thing about being the oldest man on the team. These young guys make me feel weathered beyond my years.

I mean, I'm only forty and yet I feel a hundred compared to them.

"Hollywood. You said *I guess the rumors were true.*"

"Oh." He sets his phone in his lap. "It started in boot camp and followed him throughout his career. He won't confirm or deny it, but the rumor is he's related to some old school Hollywood family. We know he's from Southern California, and there were stories at our graduation that Knox Mejer was in attendance with his family. Do you know Knox?"

"The action movie star?"

"The one with a twin brother who does all his stunt work, an older brother who is a blockbuster producer and director, and a fine as hell supermodel sister who has starred in many a young man's fantasies? That's the one."

"Okay, so why do you think Logan is related to them?"

"Well, when the stories circulated that the Mejer family was on post, we tried to figure out who they would be there to see. Then we realized we couldn't find Logan anywhere. At first, the rumor started as a joke, but what I heard from Karden was a few years later, while they were deployed overseas, the USO came through and Ms. Lyra Mejer, aka Selyne, accompanied her big brother Knox on his press tour for the movie O Five Hundred. After the show, Logan was put on a seventy-two-hour R&R, even though there were no flights in or out of the area that week. No one knew where he went."

"Bullshit." I roll my eyes.

"I'm serious."

"Why would a guy with that kind of money and those kinds of connections end up as an army grunt on the front line?"

Linc shrugs and kicks his feet up on my dash. "Don't know. Maybe he's an adrenaline junkie or a glutton for punishment?"

"Spoken like a self-flagellating adrenaline junkie," I mutter, narrowing my eyes on his feet. "Speaking of death-defying acts—if you don't get your boots off my dash, I'm going to break both of your legs."

He blanches and drops his feet to the floor. "Sorry. I forgot how you are about your truck."

I frown as he uses the sleeve of his sweatshirt to wipe away any trace of his boot prints before returning his attention to his phone.

Two hours and four how-to podcast episodes later, we make it to the resort without issue. The roads are clear and the sun hovers just above the horizon—the sky a clear crystal blue overhead. It promises an amazing and warm soft-opening, but I've been up here enough to know better than to believe the sky for an accurate weather report. Radar says a mild storm will roll through tomorrow afternoon, but we'll see if that really happens and if it will be mild or not.

I park my big truck near the staff dormitory and kill the engine before nudging Linc awake. I swear, the guy can fall asleep anywhere.

"Are we here?" He runs his hand down his face.

"Yeah. Leave your bag, but bring your skis. Let's check in and get our keys and assignments for tomorrow."

"Cool." He jumps out of his seat and opens the back door, leashing Li-Lou with her service vest and grabbing his gear.

I lift Sarge out of the back and put her paws on solid ground before grabbing my gear. The four of us walk through the front door of the lodge and take a left through the ski equipment rental shop to the staff door secured by an electronic keypad entry.

A lyrical laugh trickles through the air and tickles the back of my neck as I pull up the text message with this year's security code.

"Holy shit," Linc hisses.

"What?" I turn to look over my shoulder.

Two blondes, one curvier than the other, both equally beautiful with sun-kissed skin, sit on the bench next to the rental counter. They giggle with unburdened joy as one attempts to yank the hard cast rental boot off the other.

"Do you think they're sisters?" Linc damn near growls and I can't help but pin him with a shake of my head.

"Don't know. Why?"

"We should ask them out."

I punch the code into the keypad and the lock pops free. "No."

"Why not?"

"Sweet Jesus." I mutter, leading the way inside the staff area with Sarge by my side. Linc follows, but stays standing in the doorway looking out at the women like a kid outside of a store gazing longing through the display window at the prized toy of the season. "To be a young horn dog full of self-confidence again."

"One, I'm not a horn dog, but fully aware of what I

like—and blondes with beautiful smiles do it for me. Secondly, when's the last time you had sex? And thirdly, what's the harm in asking them out?"

Raising my brow, I'm torn between chewing his ass and answering him honestly. While he worked for me in the military, I recruited Linc on my way out the door, unsure if he was going to re-enlist or not. There was a time when Linc was my problem child—one of my best trainers with the worst conduct off-duty. He had a lot of childhood trauma to work through when he was younger, his impulse control damn near zero when I met him.

He's grown a lot over the years.

Now, I have to remember we are colleagues, not NCO and subordinate. I outrank no one—thank god— and I like it that way.

Narrowing my eyes, I glance out at the two beautiful blondes. "You might not be a horn dog today, but I've known you since you were nineteen years old, so don't act like you've always been sweet and innocent. Secondly, my sex life is none of your business and you better never ask me about it again. And lastly, we can't date them. It's part of our employment contract that we don't ask out the resort guests."

He frowns and brings his eyes to me. "Really? I agreed to that crap?"

I shrug, a pang of disappointment settling in my belly. He isn't wrong. They are beautiful, especially the curvy one sitting on the bench. She's probably too young for me, not that I'll ever find out. Even if she isn't, I wouldn't know how to approach her anyway, much less ask her out. Being smooth with the ladies has never been my forte. "It's a fraternization thing."

"Fine. If we see them on Sunday after we get off work, we'll ask them out."

"And then what?" I scoff. "They're renting their equipment, which means they're not local. They're probably flying back to Southern California or Florida or some other beachfront property next week."

"Man," Linc grumbles and pushes past me into the locker room. "You're bumming me out."

I glance at the women one more time before turning my back and walking to the offices where our dorm keys wait for us. "You're better off finding a woman in Spring City if a relationship is what you're looking for."

He sighs, throwing his jacket and checking his gear that he left two weeks ago in his assigned locker. "I don't know what I'm looking for. I figure when I find it, I'll know."

Nodding, I hand him one of the two keys to our shared room. I've heard that's how it happens for some guys, but I myself have never been hit by Cupid's javelin.

For a man who has been married and divorced, that's saying something.

"Maybe you'll be lucky and it'll smack you upside the head with a two-by-four."

"Is that how it was for you?"

Frowning, I shake my head. "No. I don't think everyone gets a lightning bolt. I certainly never did."

At forty years old, I assume I never will.

VETERAN
K9
TEAM
REPORTING
FOR DUTY

Chapter Two
Betty

One of the most common things I hear Colorado natives say to pretty much anyone willing to listen is '*If you don't like the weather, wait five minutes*'. As a recent transplant coming from a different type of desert, I have to work hard to not roll my eyes anytime I hear it.

Two months ago, I moved to Spring City, Colorado for the job of a lifetime. Working for Taylor & Morvick PR Firm, I'll use my communications degree to set myself up for a career that I hope to love. Plus, for a smaller firm, their compensation and benefits package is top-notch. I went from making seventy thousand dollars a year straight out of college in Phoenix to making almost double in a city with a comparable cost of living.

Can you say high roller?

This is my first holiday away from home. Actually, it's my first time doing anything away from home, considering I went to ASU and lived with my mom through all four years of school. We couldn't afford dormitory living on top of my tuition and that's with scholarships and grants. It's not like I missed out, anyway. I had all the freedom I needed and the same responsibilities I would have had if I lived on campus.

My mom, who might have worse separation anxiety than me, came to visit for Thanksgiving and Christmas. I only moved to Colorado in September, so we haven't been apart for a full three months.

And yet, I'm so glad she's here. We're spending a long weekend splurging at a plush VRBO private residence up the road from the ski village at Silver Mountain.

This is a big deal in so many ways. We've never had the disposable income to rent a mini-mansion on a ski slope, much less the dollars to afford lift tickets and ski equipment.

But now...

Thank you, Taylor & Morvick!

"What happened to the clear skies we drove under yesterday?" My mom looks out the big bay window over-looking the ski lifts, where I'm curled up while slurping my second cup of coffee. Yesterday, we drove through the mountain pass under beautiful, blue skies. There was no wind, and it was nearly thirty-five degrees.

Last night, the sky was also clear. So when I tell you the stars were heavenly, I don't have the words to do it justice, which is too bad considering catchy ad copy is on the list of things I'm supposed to do for a living.

Don't tell my bosses.

I sigh. "I told you, they say if you don't like the weather, wait five minutes."

She giggles. "I thought you hate it when they say that."

"I do. It's obnoxious."

"But is it true?" She takes my cup of coffee out of my hand and takes a sip.

I frown, snatching my mug back. "Probably."

"Are we risking the ski slopes this morning?" My mom checks my hip, forcing me to scoot over so she can sit next to me.

"Well, I have my ski lesson at eleven, and I can't come up with a good reason to cancel."

"Good. The sooner you learn how to ski, the sooner we'll be hitting the slopes together. I'll get changed."

We are Arizona girls and this is the first time I have ever been knee-deep in snow. Obviously, I've seen it from afar. I think we might've even got a fluke snow storm once that accumulated like a half an inch—we attempted to make a pitiful snowman out of it, but of course, as soon as we touched the snow it melted—but my mom grew up in Northern Utah when she was a kid and loves the snow.

For twenty-three years it's been she and I. There was a man at one time, but the sperm donor took off before I could hold my head up on my own. My mom was young when she had me, seventeen and barely out of high school. The first thing my father did when they found out she was pregnant was move her as far away from her family as possible.

In retrospect, I suppose the move was a good thing,

considering both my mother and father's families are jackasses who wanted nothing to do with her after she became a teenage mother.

They actually blamed her for seducing him—a twenty year old seduced by a seventeen year old vixen. Can you believe it?

So that tells you everything you need to know about my grandparents.

It's been the two of us for the last twenty-three years. When I was growing up, my mom didn't date, didn't bring men around, and spent all of her time and attention on me. In a lot of ways, she's my older sister and my best friend, as well as my mom. We've been attached at the hip my whole life and I know she sacrificed a lot to give me, what I consider, a perfect life.

Life hasn't always been easy, but we made it work, and now I'd love for her to find a special man who will treat her like the queen she is. She deserves love and affection, and part of the reason I took a job away from home was to give her the freedom to pursue a relationship that will hopefully heal all of her old wounds.

Will I miss her? Yes.

But the two of us need to get on with our lives.

"Hurry up, Betty. Your lesson may not be until eleven, but we can use the time at the lodge to see what kind of yummies they have on the menu for later."

"Your sweet tooth and my ass need to break up." I roll my eyes and carry my coffee cup to the kitchen sink.

She smacks my butt. "Sweetheart, there's nothing

wrong with your ass. I could bounce a quarter off of your butt."

"Well, I'm glad you think so, because something tells me I'm going to be on it a lot today."

"Pish posh." She waves me away. "A couple of lessons and you'll be skiing with me in no time."

I shake my head as I close my bedroom door. "We can hope."

Twenty minutes later, I have on more layers of clothing than I think I've had on in my entire life. Cuddle duds—tops and bottoms. Two layers of socks, a fleece sweater, some kind of waterproof overalls—I think the rental staff called them bibs—another cable knit sweater over that, and a ski jacket. My hat, oversized sunglasses, and gloves are in my pockets. I'm already red-faced and breaking out into a sweat walking up the ramp to the lodge's front door.

"I think I have on too many clothes," I grumble.

"You'll be fi—" My mom takes one look at my red face and tries to suppress her smile "—ohhh... maybe you can take off your jacket and stuff it in the locker when you get hot."

I look at the gray skies that seem to get darker as the morning creeps toward noon. "You know, you should get a couple of runs in now. We may not have all afternoon to ski."

She nods. "I was thinking the same thing. Are you sure you'll be okay by yourself?"

I chuckle. "Mom, I'm twenty-three years old and

completely capable of ignoring people by scrolling TikTok on my phone while sitting near the fire in a ski lodge—similar to what I would do at a coffee shop in Spring City."

She casts me a disappointed purse of her lips. "We need to work on your social skills."

My mouth falls open. "Who are you talking to?"

Chuckling, she nods. "Okay. We need to work on *our* social skills. I'm going to get on the lift and tackle this mountain. I will see you in forty-five minutes."

"Sounds perfect."

"**A**re you Betty?"

I look up from my phone to what I can only describe as a silver fox looming over me. This man has a youthful face, but his short hair and soft beard have silver sprinkled through the light brown fawn. As soon as I bring my gaze up to meet him, his forest green eyes sparkle with his gentle smile, and a ball of ooey-gooey warmth hits me in the gut.

God, this man is beautiful.

It's been a long time since a wave of instant attraction has hit me in the belly like this.

"I am. Are you my torturer for the day?" My caustic tongue throws the words out before my brain can stop them.

His smile widens. "Are you looking to be tortured?"

A handful of responses, none of which are appropriate, run through my brain.

Why not?

By you, yes.

What do you have in mind?

Instead, I press my lips together and move to stand up, struggling to get my knees and elbows to bend with all the material strangling them in place. I swear I have on so many clothes, something easy like standing is taxing my energy reserves.

He grabs a hold of my biceps and pulls me to my feet. We're standing so close I can smell the clean scent of his soap and a hint of cologne, or aftershave, or maybe it's body wash. Whatever it is, it's got a spicy masculine scent that makes me want to lean in and press my nose to his neck.

Would inhaling deeply make me a pervert? Maybe.

Would he welcome it anyway?

"You seem to have on a lot of layers." He steadies me on my feet, both of his hands gripping my upper arms.

Biting my lip, I tilt my head back to look up at him. He's tall, at least six-three, and towers over my five-foot-five frame. "Too many, honestly, but I'm afraid to take off the jacket because I don't think I can get it back on if I do. Do you remember the kid from that one Christmas movie where the mom dresses him for school and he falls down and can't get back up? Yeah, I feel like that."

He chuckles, a rumble coming from his wide chest. "First time in the snow?"

"Is it that obvious?"

"Well, anyone who has played in the snow knows how quickly they overheat with exertion. Since it's just you and me today on the bunny hill, if you get hot, I'll undress you." The tip of his tongue strokes the edge of his incisor as he takes a step back.

He looks at me like I'm dessert, but with this many clothes on, I'm sure he's confused about what is me and what is packaging. I mean, I look like an abominable snowman. "Don't let the multiple layers fool you. This is all me underneath."

"You look perfect."

Good grief. I thought I was hot before. This guy has my insides on fire. "Are you going to tell me your name?"

"Barron." He offers his hand. "Nice to meet you. Are you ready to head outside?"

I slip my phone into my breast pocket and shake his perfectly calloused hand, making me wonder what he does when he's not teaching toddlers and desert dwellers how to spend the day on their asses. "Let's get this over with."

"We'll have fun. I promise. The notes said you had your gear fitted yesterday?"

"Yes."

"Great. Let's head to the top of the bunny hill."

We go over some basics: clipping into and popping out of the skis, duck walking and side stepping, maintaining balance, how to turn, how to stop, how to hold the poles.

"Ready for the hard part?" Barron smiles, his eyes going up to the sky.

"Go that way—" I point down the hill "—really fast?"

"Nope." He shakes his head and then does something completely unexpected by pushing me onto my butt.

"Hey!"

"I'm going to teach you how to stand up in your skis."

For the next ten minutes, he explains how to position my skis and use my poles to stand up, but it is not happening. I'm hot, sweaty, frustrated—and embarrassed by my clear lack of athletic prowess.

"It's okay, Betty. I have another way for you to get up."

He has me roll onto my belly and position my skis in a way that I can come up on my knees. This position feels a lot more stable and the sense of pride and achievement I have when I finally stand up on my own must be clear on my face because he flashes me the biggest smile.

"Hey," a guy at the bottom of the hill calls up.

Barron waves and the guy rides the magic carpet up and then skis down to us.

This guy is closer to my age and just as handsome, but without the raw ruggedness that my instructor rocks. He's wearing the same Silver Mountain jacket Barron has on, but his Velcro patch says Search & Rescue instead of Instructor.

He nods at me, his lips tilted in a wry smile. "How's it going?"

"I successfully stood up on my own." I offer, because

what else can I possibly say about this entire experience? It's the only achievement I have.

"That's half the battle. You'll be on the slopes in no time."

Smiling, I look from him to Barron, who watches me closely. "Yeah, that's what I'm told."

"Forgive my intrusion, but we're closing down the mountain. The storm is rolling in faster than expected and we're trying to get everybody sheltered." He looks at Barron and then back at me. "You were with another woman earlier. Was that your sister?"

He saw us earlier?

Did they both see us earlier?

"My sister? No. That's my mother."

"Your mother?" He seems genuinely surprised, but quickly shakes it off. "Do you know where she is right now?"

"No. She took the lifts up, but I don't know which path she took."

"Do you think she would've gone back to the condo or is waiting for you in the lodge?"

Shaking my head adamantly, a touch of fear tightens my belly. "No. If she had skied down, she would've come straight to this hill to watch my lesson."

He nods, exchanging a glance with Barron. "How good of a skier is she?"

I shrug. "I think she was fantastic when she was a kid, but it's been twenty years."

"Okay. There's nothing to worry about. I'm sure she'll be down any minute." He turns to Barron. "The team's heading up to clear the mountain, but if she checks in, let me know."

"Okay. Are you taking Li-Lou?"

"Yeah, I think I might." He turns back to me again. "What's your mom's name?"

"Brandi."

VETERAN
K9
TEAM

REPORTING
FOR DUTY

Chapter Three
Barron

"Should I be worried?" Betty—a vision with her strawberry-blonde hair, flushed red cheeks, and big black-rimmed sunglasses—looks up at me after Linc skies away.

As if to answer her, a big gust of wind blows through the valley, announcing the storm to everyone near the lodge and ski lifts.

"No, but I think you should hang out with me until we find her or she finds you. Does she have her phone on her?"

"Yeah, she does." Betty pulls her phone out of her pocket and dials. She lets it ring until it goes to voicemail. "Hey. Call me as soon as you get this. I need to know you're okay. I'll be waiting for you in the lodge."

"Don't worry too much, Betty. The signal isn't great on top of the mountain, or she might be skiing and can't pick up her phone."

She nods. "You're right. I know you're right."

"Do you want to finish your lesson or are you done for the day?" It doesn't take a rocket scientist to know Betty's not overly excited about learning to ski.

"I think I'm done."

I smile. "Would you like to grab coffee or hot cocoa with me while we wait? You could tell me about yourself."

"What do you want to know?" Her left brow arches above her frames.

"Everything."

"Really? You want to know everything about me?"

"Is that wrong?"

She purses her lips. "Wrong? No. Surprising? Yes."

"I don't know why it's surprising. You're a beautiful woman who has a story to tell. Plus, with the mountain shutting down, you can't tell me you don't have the time." Shrugging my shoulders to play it cool, I motion between us with a casual wave of my hand and flash her a sweet smile. "What do you say? Me, you and a couple mugs of hot chocolate?"

"That sounds divine." She returns my smile and is even more beautiful than I thought she was the moment I laid eyes on her yesterday. Now that I know Brandi is Betty's mother and not her sister, I'm betting she is closer in age to Linc than me.

Hell, she might be young enough to be my daughter, if I'd ever had one.

Well, shit. That complicates things, doesn't it?

After we grabbed dinner last night, Linc and I racked out in our bunks with our dogs settled on their pillows.

We watched a movie, but honestly I couldn't tell you what it was about, much less the title. Linc's question about my sex life and his conviction that *when he found the one, he'd know it* had my brain spinning until I passed out from sheer exhaustion. At forty years old, you'd think I'd have been in love a couple times, but I haven't. At least, not the kind of love that left me feeling like I can't breathe without her—whoever she is.

My ex-wife is a good woman and there is no ill-will between us. We were friends in high school and reconnected many years later online while I was deployed overseas. She was looking for a way out of Branson and had romanticized what life as a military spouse would look like based on all the travel I had done. I had nothing else going on, so I invited her to come see me in Georgia.

Next thing I knew, we were married and setting up a home.

I know boredom is a stupid reason for getting married, but at the time neither of us thought we needed the passion that a deeply in love couple shares. We believed friendship would be enough. Eventually, she wanted the stability of setting roots in one place—turns out that moving every couple years and having to make new friends every time weighed on her—and I can't say I blame her.

I spent all night thinking about that relationship and my lack of romantic connection. They say love will find you when you're not looking, but in my case, I think I've been actively ignoring it my whole life.

What would happen if I paid attention and made myself available?

What would happen if I opened myself up to rejection, found the hot blonde I fantasized about last night and asked her out?

As the fates would have it—I'm about to find out.

I help Betty ski down to the bottom of the bunny hill and show her how to lock and carry her skis. "Follow me, bunny."

"Bunny?" I chuckle and shake my head.

"Yeah. You need a pet name and bunny hill Betty is too long." Dammit, I should not be flirting. Now that I know I'm closer to her mother's age, all the sexy thoughts I've been thinking seem wrong. I mean, it won't stop my mind from wandering, but I feel like a dirty dog.

She walks ahead of me toward the lodge and tosses over her shoulder in a playful tone. "Fine. I'll be your bunny."

"Do you mind if we pick up my girl on our way to the hearth?"

Betty stops and looks back at me. "Your girl?"

"Yeah." I smile at the detected note of jealousy. "We're kind of inseparable. You'll like her, and I'm sure she'll like you, even though she is possessive of me."

"Uh... okay."

I walk her through the equipment rental area into the staff break room where my German Shepherd sleeps in her bed.

I open the door and Sarge lifts her head, her tail wagging slowly. "This is my girl, Sarge."

Betty gasps. "A puppy!"

"Not exactly. She's twelve years old and has been with me for a long time."

"I'm sure she's still a puppy at heart." She coos, coaxing Sarge to stand up on her achy bones. I've had her since she was three months old and although she's in great shape, she has arthritis in her joints after years of faithful service.

Sarge walks over to Betty and sits patiently in front of her. "Can I pet her?"

"She insists." I chuckle and guide Betty over to the couch. "Sit down and I will help you get off some of this gear."

As soon as Betty sits, Sarge climbs up onto the couch and lays next to her, resting her head on Betty's thigh. I envy my dog's ability to be so familiar without speaking a word and wish I could cuddle up with Betty without coming up with some clever conversation.

I'm not so great with clever conversation.

"Ohhh. She's so sweet." Betty runs her fingers through my dog's thick coat.

"Sarge is a retired military working dog, but I don't make her go out in the snow anymore than she absolutely has to." I drop to one knee in front of Betty to unbuckle her boots and pull them off.

"Ahhhh," she moans and drops her head back while wiggling her toes. "That feels so good."

The pleasurable cry escaping her lips sends blood rushing to my cock while a lightness I haven't felt in years fills my heart. I chuckle and squeeze her wool-wrapped foot, pressing my thumb to the arch. "If you're a good girl, I'll give you a foot massage later."

She stops stroking Sarge's fur and looks at me. With her glasses off, I can see her big brown eyes filled with surprise. I'm wondering if she's going to kick her foot to my face, jump up and storm off, or chew my ass for being a dirty old man.

Thankfully, her lips curl into a small smile. "I can be a good girl."

Suppressing my smile, I nod.

Game on.

If she's weirded out by our age difference, she's not letting it show. "I bet you can. Do you want to take off your coat? I'll secure it and your boots in my locker while we hang out in the lodge."

"I don't have any other shoes with me."

"I have some slippers you can wear, but you have to promise not to make fun of me for having them."

"Ohhh? I'm intrigued." She leans forward and unzips her coat.

I help her pull it off and motion to the oversized cable-knit sweater she has on underneath it. "Do you want to lose that, too?"

"I think I'll keep it with me, in case I get cold."

"Okay. I'll be right back."

"Wait." She has her hands up, and damn, I like the sight of her reaching for me. "My phone."

"Right." I hand her coat back to her. She digs her phone and wallet out of her pocket before giving it back to me. "Be right back."

In the locker room, I run into one of the mountain safety dispatchers while shedding my outer layers. "How's it going out there?"

"Fine. We have almost everyone off the mountain and accounted for." Sherry bats her lashes. "What are you going to do now that you have the afternoon and evening free?"

"Uh... I have my client in the break room waiting for her family to come down the mountain." I run my hand through my hair and fluff out the hat imprint, feeling weird about saying *mother*. That makes it sound like I have a child with me—which is who I normally instruct—instead of a very adult woman with ample curves I'd like to explore. "Speaking of which. Do you have an extra radio on you? I told Linc I'd let him know if the family shows up."

"Sure." She pulls a second radio out of her pocket. "He's on channel three. Do you want to catch up later after the family picks up their kid? I think a group of us are going hot tubbing tonight."

"Probably not, but I'll call you later if I change my mind."

I'm not going to change my mind.

Sherry's too young for me and yet she's been flirting with me since last season. I thought once I brought Linc around she'd change her focus, but nope.

Still hitting on me.

It's crazy, but it also gets me thinking. "How old are you?"

Her face brightens with the unintended flirtatious

question. "Me? I'm twenty, but I'll be twenty-one next month."

"Right." I change my boots and stuff mine and Betty's jackets into my locker. "Happy Birthday. In case I forget."

Sherry smiles and wiggles her fingers in the air as she sashays out of the locker room. "Oh, I won't let you forget me."

Frowning, I turn the radio to channel three, and press the button to talk. "Linc? Lincoln, do you copy?"

"Barron?"

"Yeah man. I got a radio, just in case. How's it look up there?"

He exhales and I can tell he's ducking his head with the radio into his coat so he can hear me. "It's hitting harder than we thought, but I think we have almost everybody off the mountain. I haven't seen Brandi yet. Is she with you?"

"No, I don't think she's checked in. I'll ask Betty and let you know shortly."

"Okay. Are you going to be hanging out with her until then?"

I glance around the locker room, thankful I'm alone. "Yeah. I convinced her to stay with me and Sarge for now."

"Good. If Brandi shows up, invite them to dinner."

Shaking my head, I roll my eyes. Linc definitely has a one track mind. "You know that Betty is closer to your age and Brandi is closer to mine."

"I don't give a shit. The moment I laid eyes on Brandi

yesterday, I wanted her. Seeing her again this morning and having Betty be your client—it's fate."

I sigh and grab the fuzzy penguin slippers out of my locker. "I'll do my best. Keep the comm line open."

"Roger. Talk to you soon."

When I enter the break room, Betty has pulled off her cable-knit sweater, but has it draped across her stomach. That action makes me think she's self-conscious about her body, which is crazy considering I saw her in leggings and a sweater yesterday and my mouth immediately watered. She has these thick thighs and perfectly round ass, and I want to applaud her Lululemon collection.

I think that's what stretch pants are called.

All I know is I'm a diehard fan of Lycra and spandex and anything else that conforms to a woman's shape.

Especially a shape like Betty's.

Sarge has made herself at home on my woman's thigh, her eyes closed and tongue lolling out of her mouth while Betty continues to stroke her fur. "Any word from Brandi?"

Betty looks up from her phone. "No. Not yet. How is it looking outside?"

"The storm is moving faster than we expected, but it will be okay. If she's in a situation where she needs to be found, there's nobody better on the mountain than Linc and Li-Lou."

"Who is Li-Lou?"

"Linc's dog. She retired with him when he separated

from the Army, just like I retired with Sarge when it was our time."

"Are you canine handlers?"

"We were and still are." I bring my hand from behind my back and show her the ridiculous slippers.

She laughs. "Why do you have those?"

I drop to my knee and slide them on her feet, a distracting desire to run my hand up her calves and between her knees to push apart her things taking root in my mind. Jesus. This isn't me. I've never been consumed by thoughts of touching or tasting a woman before, but they are coming fast and unbidden with Betty.

"A client's mother gave them to me as a gift after I charmed her little girl over her stuffed penguin ski hat."

"A hardened soldier with a viciously trained military dog—" she lifts Sarge's lips to emphasize how unafraid she is "—who schmoozes ski bunnies out of fuzzy penguin slippers on the weekends. You are a complicated man, Barron."

Shaking my head, I offer her my hand. "I'm a man, so that makes me easy to understand. It's you I want to get to know."

Sarge groans as she maneuvers off of the couch, while Betty takes my hand, letting me pull her up on her slippered feet. "Are you ready for something hot and sinful?"

Fuck it, I'm obviously not going to stop flirting, so I'm might as well lean into it.

She slips her hand into my arm and smiles up at me sweetly. "Lead the way, mystery man."

VETERAN
K9
TEAM
REPORTING
FOR DUTY

Chapter Four
Betty

I'm conflicted.

Obviously, I'm worried about my mother and want her to be safe, but at the same time, I'm enjoying my time with Barron. It's been a long time since I've been attracted to a man and I was really hoping my move to Colorado would reboot my love life, not that it was successfully running in Arizona.

Plus, I doubt he'd be flirty in front of my mother. Even though we are more like sisters—especially now that I'm an adult—in the end he'd know who she was and would probably hold his tongue.

We walk through the lodge to one of the many fireplaces, this one with a cozy little loveseat in front of it and not much else. It's off in the corner, which I guess is why nobody else has taken residence in front of it.

"You sit here and take care of my baby and I will be back with something yummy."

I grin up at him as I plop down on the uncomfortable

couch, Sarge curling up at my feet. "Yummy, huh? What happened to hot and sinful?"

"Can't it be all three?"

"I guess I'm about to find out."

"Don't get in trouble while I'm gone."

"I make no promises."

I check my phone again as he walks away and glance at the blizzard hitting the window. It seems like it's sleeting or hailing or something like that, but I can't see the mountain anymore, or the ski lifts at this point.

Where is she?

I text and then call her again, trying to keep my voice calm. Would she have gone straight back to the house?

No. Never.

But if she's not there, then where is she?

Barron approaches with a tray. "Something sweet and something savory, just in case."

On the tray is a cinnamon roll, something that looks like a banana bread and a turkey sandwich, as well as two waters and two steamy mugs of hot cocoa. "You didn't have to get us all this."

He shrugs and sits down next to me. "I want to make sure you're comfortable."

I glance out the window one more time. "Do you think she's okay?"

He also looks out the window and I can see the wheel spinning in his head. "Let me hit up Linc, again."

He pulls the radio out of his pocket, and turns the volume down so it's just for us. "Linc, do you copy?"

"Yeah."

"I have Betty sitting with me. Any luck?"

"Not yet. I'm going to go over the top of the ridge and hit the backside of the mountain."

Barron licks his lips and I can tell he's worried about saying anything in front of me that might stoke my fears or spike my anxiety. "How's the visibility up there?"

"Not great. Are you sure she didn't go back to the house?"

I shrug. "She's not answering her phone."

Barron takes in a deep breath and then lets it out slowly. "Maybe we should check?"

"Okay."

A couple minutes later, he's handing me a bag for the food and my coat. "Where are you staying?"

"A VRBO up the hill in the Silver Mountain Aspen community."

"In the private houses?" His raised brow lets me know he's very aware of the opulence on the hill.

I shrug. "We're splurging?"

"Nice splurge. How about I get my truck and pull it to the door while you stay with Sarge? I'll carry you to the truck so you don't have to put the ski boots back on. Then we'll drive to your VRBO and see if we can find your mom."

I reach out and grab his forearm before he can walk away. "Thank you for being so nice to me."

He smiles. "You're easy to be nice to."

I didn't think he meant he was going to actually pick me up, but that is exactly what he does. I wait at the front door with Sarge, as a beautiful black Ford King Ranch pulls up. Barron is a mountain of a man, but I'm a big girl, so I assumed he was going to help me traverse the ice and snow on the ground, not literally sweep me up in a fireman's hold and carry me to the passenger seat.

"Oh, my god. I cannot believe you did that."

"Did what?" he asks as he sets me down and hands me the seatbelt.

"Picked me up. The ice and snow are very dangerous."

He stops what he's doing and looks at me, his brow furrowing, his expression incredulous. "I'm a search and rescue guy. I think I know what's dangerous and what's not. You and your beautiful ass might be a danger to me, but having me carry you around is about as safe as you can get."

Reaching over me, he clicks the seatbelt into place and smiles. "Now I got you locked in, safe and sound."

He pauses, his lips close enough I could lean forward and sneak a kiss.

Dang. I really want to, too.

Dimples form in his cheeks as he presses his lips together and pulls back. He closes the door and opens the back, calling for Sarge. She walks over and jumps up with her front paws, but he has to lift her back end to get her in safely. Even though it's only a two-minute drive from the village to the house, it takes almost ten, considering the lack of visibility and the crazy people trying to leave the mountain.

"These people are going to get hurt if they drive home in this weather."

He frowns and shakes his head. "Colorado drivers. It happens all the time. They're trying to beat the CDOT before they close down the highway. If they can make it to the tunnel, they'll be fine. I bet it's not even snowing on the other side of the mountain."

"Really? That happens here?"

"The Eisenhower Tunnel? Absolutely. It can be a blizzard on one side and a perfectly sunny day on the other."

"Wow."

He pulls up to the mini-mansion's four-car garage. Unwilling to risk losing the keys, I have the garage door opener in my jacket. One click and the door opens with more than enough room for his big truck.

"Garage parking? My truck isn't used to such luxury."

I giggle. "It's a lot of house for two people, but it had all the posh requirements for our girls getaway weekend."

"What requirements are those?"

"Hot tub, fireplace, mountain views, and two luxury bedrooms. You see, I just moved here, and I really wanted to pamper my mom for the holidays."

"Sounds like heaven."

"Yeah." I realize she hasn't come to the door yet, which tells me she's not here.

Exiting the vehicle, I enter the house and call for my mom. There's no answer and I feel myself getting upset as Barron walks up behind me and wraps his fingers around the back of my neck, massaging gently and soothing me instantly. "It'll be okay. Linc will not fail her, you, or me."

As if the ski gods knew we needed them, his radio squawks.

"Barron?"

"I read you."

"I got her, but I don't think we're going to make it down the mountain."

"Why? What's going on?" Barron's worried gaze lands on me.

"She's fine. She's right here—" his voice gets muffled as he says something to my mom and her voice comes over the radio.

I sigh in relief.

"Betty?"

"Mom, are you okay?"

"I'm fine. I'm pissed, but I'm fine."

"What happened to you?"

She growls and I can picture her rolling her eyes. "Short story: I overestimated my abilities, went to the top of the lifts, got turned around in the blizzard and ended up on the backside of the mountain."

Linc cuts in. "We're at Ranger Station Twelve."

Barron nods his understanding. "And you guys can't make it down the mountain?"

"Possibly could, but I don't want to risk it," Linc says.

"Any medical needs?" Barron replies.

"Negative."

Their clipped conversation reeks of ex-military

jargon. Two men who communicate all the details they need in little more than grunts and head nods.

I wonder if there's something they're not telling me?

"I'm sorry for ruining our game night," my mom calls from a distance.

"It's fine, Mom." I roll my eyes. "We can play tomorrow."

Barron has a quizzical look on his face, so I know I'll be explaining it to him shortly. "Are you sure you don't need anything?"

Linc responds. "Conditions are near white out up here and according to dispatch, the weather is only going to get worse over the next couple of hours. I got a fire going and basic provisions on me, so we'll be good until the morning."

"Okay. I'll keep the line open in case you need me."

"Roger. We'll be fine."

Barron sets his radio down on the counter and looks at me. "You okay?"

I shrug. "From what I can tell, Mom is not coming home tonight, but she's safe and warm and presumably with a man who, if he had to, could kill a bear to save her life."

At least that's what I'm going to assume search and rescue does on a wild Colorado mountaintop.

He nods. "That about sums Linc up. I guess you're stuck with me for the evening—if you want to be?"

I unzip my coat and shed the many layers I have on. "Are you flirting with me?"

"Has that not been obvious?" He grins.

I giggle. "No, it's pretty obvious."

"Oh good. It's been a long time, so I thought I was rusty."

"It's been a long time since you flirted?"

"Yeah, I don't do it a lot."

"Why not?"

"I haven't been inspired."

"Why me?"

He shakes his head, his eyes going to the giant window overlooking the ski resort that is currently invisible—nothing more than a blanket of white. "I don't know. You're beautiful, but that isn't usually enough for me to flirt. Maybe it's your infectious laughter I heard yesterday?"

"You heard me laughing yesterday?"

"Oh yes. Linc and I both noticed you and your... mom almost immediately."

"You're having a hard time with the fact that she's my mother and not my sister, aren't you?"

He shrugs and unbuttons his coat. "It means I'm old enough to be your father."

"That's not a problem for me. Is it a problem for you?"

His dark green eyes sparkle as his lips spread into a wicked smile. "I have no problems."

"Good. Are you hungry?"

"Are you inviting me to stay for dinner?"

"Wasn't that obvious?"

"Does that mean I get to join game night, too?"

I raise my brow in challenge. "You don't know what

game we're playing."

He shrugs, his eyes glued to mine. "I doubt I'll care, as long as I'm playing with you."

Naked Twister it is.

We've held intense eye contact for over a minute, but that cheesy line makes me laugh and roll my eyes. "Whatever."

Barron cups my cheek before I can turn away. "Don't discount my enthusiasm to spend a snowy day locked indoors with a beautiful woman. I don't care what we do. I'm just happy to be spending time with you, Betty."

Oh man—I need to shed layers because my insides are burning up. "I'm going to change. I'd offer you some clothes, but..."

"I have a bag in the truck, if you're okay with me also changing into something more comfortable."

"Of course, get as comfortable as you want." I point at a door behind him. "There's a bedroom over there."

"I'd love a tour. I've never been in a multi-million dollar home before."

"You're on." I grab our jackets and hang them on the hooks near the mudroom door. Standing at the base of the stairs, I glance over my shoulder and throw him a flirty wink. "I'll meet you here in ten minutes."

Quickly climbing to the second-floor bedrooms, I pull my cable-knit sweater over my head and shuck the over-alls of my pants off my shoulders.

Shedding my clothes, I walk into the bathroom with my mind fixated on the last time I shaved my legs.

Let's face it, I really want to kiss Barron and I'm

pretty sure he wants to kiss me—and if we kiss, there's a good possibility we're going to do more. Considering the last time I've worried about a man touching my bare legs was forever ago, I'm not the best at making sure I shave my legs every day.

Not since I moved away from a city with an infinite supply of short wearing days.

I take one look in the mirror at the mascara rings around my eyes and dried sweat plastering my hair in different directions, and can't believe this man's been flirting with me at all.

How embarrassing.

I strip my clothes and turn on the shower, quickly washing my face and hair before shaving my legs. The hot water feels amazing and definitely has me looking forward to hot tubbing later.

I wonder if Barron would want to soak with me?

I've never jacuzzi'd with a man before, but it sounds sinfully perfect. We didn't have one in Arizona and hot tubs aren't necessarily the most popular items when you live in a place that is typically over one hundred degrees, but the idea of being near naked, bubbles and jets pounding your body while also being pounded into...

Hot!

I'll have to figure out how to slip it into the conversation—and soon.

VETERAN
K9
TEAM

REPORTING
FOR DUTY

Chapter Five
Barron

Donning the pair of gray sweatpants and long sleeve Henley I had in my bag, I grab Sarge's bed and blanket, as well as her food bowl, out of the truck and set up a spot for her near the fire. I'm not sure this house allows dogs, but at her age, she doesn't cause much trouble anymore.

She does shed all year long, so I'll keep her off of the furniture this one time to protect Betty's damage deposit.

I'm glad Brandi is okay and Linc found her, but something tells me he was not telling us the full story over the radio. The mom seemed cryptic too, and I'm wondering if she's hurt. Obviously, she's not critically injured, or else Linc would never risk her well-being by refusing an emergency evacuation.

Maybe he's hoping to spend some time with her—a little forced proximity where the two of them have no choice but to get to know each other. Not that Linc would do that on purpose, but he would jump at the chance if it was available.

Am I any better, using the storm and Betty's missing mother as an opportunity to offer my company?

No. I suppose I'm not.

Betty comes down the stairs with wet hair, polar bear pajama bottoms, and a soft fuzzy sweater. She scrubbed her face clean and absolutely glows with touchable softness. "You took a shower?"

"How could you not tell me I had mascara down to my cheekbones?" She strikes a pose with her hands on her hips, which pulls her sweater tight against her puckered nipples.

I shake my head and cast my eyes down, because god damn, the vision of her makes my mouth water. "I honestly didn't notice."

"I'm not sure if I should be flattered or offended."

"Flattered?" I grin and bring my head up. "I think you're beautiful, no matter what."

She drops her hands and takes a few steps toward me. "You know, you don't have to keep calling me beautiful. You're already in the house."

I close the space between us, waiting until she tilts her head back to look up at me. "Let's get one thing straight, bunny. I'm not blowing smoke up your ass. If I say you're beautiful, it means I find you fucking breathtaking, and you're going to have to accept that."

Betty licks her lips. "Oh."

"Yeah." My gaze goes to her pouty lips before coming back up to her eyes. "Oh."

She sucks in her breath. "Do you want that tour now?"

In my head I'm screaming *'No, I don't want a fucking tour. I want to lay you out on this countertop and fucking feast.'*

Instead, I nod my head. "Yeah, give me the tour."

She walks me through the ground floor. Two smaller bedrooms, a ski in/ski out mudroom and a glass-enclosed hot tub with an adjoining sauna. Kitchen, living room, and a private office complete the main level—everything tastefully decorated and made for VRBO hospitality.

We're climbing the ornate staircase when Betty reaches out and intertwines her fingers with my hand. "Do you live on the mountain all year, or somewhere else during the summer?"

Heat travels up my arm from the simple touch, our joined hands feeling more than natural—it's comforting, like I'm finally home. "I live and work in Spring City. We're only up here on the weekends when we're scheduled to work. It's a nice perk—free housing and skiing—and it's a nice break from the kennels. Plus, once you get on the mountain's payroll, you don't want to fall off."

"I live in Spring City. I moved there in September from Phoenix."

"What brought you to town?"

"A great job with the PR firm Taylor & Morvick."

"What do you do for them?"

"I'm on the social media management team. I study the platform algorithms and trending designs and help build catchy advertisements for our clients."

"So that's why you're on your phone all the time."

She blushes a bit. "I know it's annoying. My mom hates it too."

That stings a little, but I try to blow it off. "Not annoying, but I guess I won't take it personally if you feel the need to check your phone often while we're hanging out."

Her eyes sparkle as she looks into mine. "All you have to do is give me a reason to put it down, and I will."

"Where is your phone right now?"

She beams. "Downstairs on the counter."

"Mmmm. Good girl."

She gushes under my praise, something I'm very aware of as it speaks to the dominant streak within me.

Good girl works for her.

I wonder what else will?

We arrive at the landing at the top of the stairs. She points to the left. "Upstairs, there are four bedrooms, two of which are primary suites. There's also two smaller bedrooms in the middle with a Jack-and-Jill separating them. The one to the left is my mother's room, and this one is mine."

This is moving fast, our mutual attraction so palpable, I can taste it on my tongue. I know I should slow this down, yet I can't stop the words from spilling from my lips. "Are you going to show me your bedroom, Betty?"

She bites her lip. "If you want to see it."

"I definitely want to see it."

She walks forward, pulling me behind her with our hands still joined.

I feel like a kid. My gut tightens into a ball, anticipation and excitement warring for dominance in my body.

The bedroom is posh opulence at its finest. There's a huge king-size bed against one wall—and the wall to the left is pure glass windows overlooking the mountain. Across from the bed is an enormous fireplace with two chairs sitting in front of it. On the fourth wall is an open archway into the en suite bathroom. Leaning against the wall next to the door is a giant mirror—at least seven feet tall by five feet wide—giving me all kinds of filthy ideas.

Laid across the floor is a large sheepskin rug—white and fluffy—but if I had my way, I'd move it in front of the hearth so we could stretch out on it in front of a roaring fire.

"Damn. So this is how the one percent lives, huh?"

"I don't have this kind of money. We've done nothing like this before."

"I didn't say that as a jab to you, Betty, but could you imagine coming home to this every day?"

She shakes her head. "I couldn't imagine having to clean it every day."

I snort. "I don't think people who live in houses like this clean them themselves."

She giggles. "True."

Wiggling her fingers, she mosves to let go of my hand, but I can't have that. I pull her fingers to my lips, kissing each tip gently. "What games do you want to play?"

Shaking her head, she glues her eyes to my lips. "I think there are some board games downstairs."

"What does the winner get?"

"I guess that would depend on who the winner is."

"What if I won? What would I get?"

"What do you want?"

I grin. "How about a kiss?"

"You don't have to lose to me for that."

Damn. That's all I needed to hear.

I pull her into my arms, snaking my hand around her waist while I slide the other into her hair. We press our bodies together, but I hold back on claiming her mouth, taking a moment to stare into her big brown eyes while trying to convey my thoughts without having to say the words.

Tell me to stop.

Tell me this is too fast.

Tell me I'm a dirty old man and I shouldn't be touching you like this.

Of course, I say none of these things.

She lifts on her toes, touching the tip of her nose to mine. "Are you going to claim your prize?"

"I have done nothing to deserve a prize yet."

"You taught me how to stand up on skis today, gave me penguin slippers and sinfully delicious hot chocolate, all the while helping to ensure my mom is safe."

"Good point. I guess I deserve a little something." I kiss her gently, pressing my lips softly against hers at first. It only takes one moan from Betty, her eyes fluttering close as she sinks into my embrace, and any semblance of control I have flies out the window.

She grips my biceps and urges me on, parting her lips

with a soft sigh. I slip my tongue into her mouth and pull her tighter against my body.

Our tongues tangle as my hand slips down to cup her plump ass, pulling her even tighter against my hardening cock. "Oh fuck, I knew you would be sweet."

"Don't stop, Barron."

"What are you saying, bunny?"

She looks me in the eye, her gaze unwavering in her conviction. "I'm saying it's been a long time since somebody has touched me. I don't want you to stop."

"Is this a secret one-time thing, Betty, or are we open to more?"

"Secret?" Her brow furrows, letting me know she has no idea what I'm talking about.

"We're one hundred miles away from home and your mother is out for the evening. I'm wondering if this is a one-time thing or would you let me take you to dinner in Spring City?"

Her smile is electric. "You're asking me out."

It's a statement, not a question.

"Yes."

"I'd love to go out with you."

"Good." I lean forward and claim her lips again, letting my hands slide down her back, cupping and pulling her ass against me again. I back her up until her thighs hit the mattress, and she has no choice but to sit down.

Reaching behind my head, I yank off my Henley and toss it on the floor beside me.

She sucks in her breath, her eyes lighting up as they move over my body. "Damn."

I'm a mountain man with a lot of silver speckled chest hair and considering I'm at least fifteen years older than her, I'm wondering if she's been with somebody built like me. Not knowing makes me a bit self-conscious. "What does *damn* mean?"

She slides her fingers through the hair on my chest, circling and flicking my nipple with her thumb. "You are all man, Barron—" a blush hits her cheeks. "What's your last name?"

"Theroux. What's yours?"

"Appleton."

In my head, I'm thinking Betty Theroux sounds better, but I'm obviously not going to say that.

Sliding my fingers underneath the bottom of her sweater, I lift gently. She raises her arms over her head for me, making it easy to pull both her sweater off, leaving her bare for my gaze.

Fuck me, I knew she had full breasts, but she's perfect for a man my size.

I cup her drool-worthy, mouthwatering flesh in my hands, barely able to contain her. "You are perfect."

Betty isn't shy, reaching forward to stroke my erection through my sweatpants.

I groan, tilting my face to the ceiling and closing my eyes. Her touch is authoritative and demanding, telling me she knows exactly what she wants.

Me.

Fuck, this is going to happen.

I haven't been this excited about a woman in a long time and I never expected to meet somebody here on the slopes. I usually avoid the women on the mountain because we have nothing in common. Anyone who can afford to live up here is outside my price bracket, not that I'm some slouch. I do well enough, but not million-dollar condos at the ski resort well.

She reaches into my sweatpants and pulls out my cock, the cool air hitting the pre-cum dripping from the head. But that doesn't matter, because then she's wrapping her lips around me, the heat from her mouth pure fucking heaven.

"Oh fuck," I hiss, looking down to find my woman swallowing me as deep as she can. I slide my hand into her hair, fighting an impulse to fist her strawberry-blonde locks and fuck her pretty mouth.

"God damn, Betty."

"Do you like it?"

"You feel fucking amazing."

"You have a nice cock worthy of worship."

And with those eight words, I can't control myself. I fist my hand in her hair and pull her off of me, picking her up and throwing her back on the bed. I'm on my knees between her legs in seconds, pulling her pajama pants down before she stops bouncing, and pushing her thighs apart to find her pussy glistening with her arousal. "Did sucking my cock get you hot?"

"Yes."

"Are you going to come for me when I fuck you with my tongue?"

"Yes."

"Good girl."

I dive in with the vigor of a starved man put in front of a buffet, licking and sucking on her slit until her engorged clit throbs for me. She rides my face with wanton abandon, her fingers digging into my hair, her nails scraping against my scalp.

"Yes, Barron. Please, right there. Don't stop. Please don't stop. Oh my God." She explodes, her thighs clamping down on my head, legs shaking as her arousal floods my mouth. She's fucking sweet, like pineapple, and I'm not sure I'll ever get enough of her taste on my tongue.

VETERAN
K9
TEAM

REPORTING
FOR DUTY

Chapter Six
Betty

Holy shit. I've never come like that before in my life.

Would he believe me if I told him?

I've been brazen this afternoon, totally unwilling to back down from what I want, which is not my normal MO.

It's not that I'm shy. I never have been, but I am careful with my mind, heart and body—so jumping into a bed with a man I met hours ago is not normal.

And yet, I want what I want.

Right now, I want Barron—here and now.

He climbs up my body and kisses me possessively, the taste of my cum on his tongue. "You are fucking delicious."

I smack my lips. "I guess I am."

He smiles. "I could feast on you every day."

"It looks like we're setting up more than one date."

He still has on his sweatpants, although his cock is

out and pressed between my legs, hard and heavy. "Are you going to fuck me now, Barron?"

He sighs. "I want to. Christ, do I fucking want to. But this isn't something I normally do, and I don't have condoms with me."

Worrying my lip, I go for broke, hoping my desperate need to have him does not turn him off. "I haven't been with anyone in over a year and a half and according to my last GYN appointment, I'm disease free."

"A year and a half? That's a long time."

"Yeah, it is. So you understand when I say I really want you to fuck me right now."

"Are you on birth control?"

"Yes."

Barron closes his eyes as if he's in pain. "Oh Betty, I'm going to fuck you so good that you'll want to come home with me."

I don't doubt him, because I already kind of do. The fact he lives in Spring City opens up so many possibilities for the future. Do we embark on a traditional relationship or will we be relegated to friends-with-benefits? Starting off hot and heavy like this, I suppose anything is possible.

He grips his cock and looks down between our bodies, slowly pushing himself in.

He's big enough to make me gasp as I arch my back and spread my legs wide. "Oh! Oh, Barron." I tilt my head back and close my eyes, soaking in the feeling of every nerve ending firing to life.

"Open up, bunny." His voice is deeper now,

demanding and gentle at the same time. "I want your eyes on me as I make love to you."

Love?

Yeah, this definitely feels like more than a quick fuck. He is slow and intentional with his movements, filling me and then withdrawing at an excruciatingly tender pace, only to fill me again, pushing a little harder each time— making me feel him deep inside of me.

I am wet.

Soaking wet.

Gushing with every stroke—in a way I've never done before.

"Fuck." Barron bites his lip. "You feel so fucking good —it's taking all of my strength to control myself."

I slide my arms around his back, gripping his shoulder blades as his muscles flex, arching my breast up into his chest. "This feels fantastic, but you can fuck me hard, too. We have all night. We can do it all."

"We have more than tonight, but let's worry about tomorrow in the morning." He lifts my leg with his powerful forearm, spreading me wider and plunging in deeper.

"Oh, god," I gasp, overwhelmed with pleasure. It's too much and I feel like I'm going to explode. I'm teetering on the edge, but unable to push over, my nerves buzzing with anticipation. "Please, Barron. Harder."

"I can feel you clench around me, bunny. Are you ready to come?"

"Yes."

He kisses me hard, disconnecting my brain from the

pressuring building in my pussy. I melt underneath him, my body his to command as he sees fit. "Fuck, you fit me perfectly."

"Mmmhmmm. We do feel amazing together, don't we?" I close my eyes for a second, opening them as soon as he slows down.

He grins, as if he caught me with my hand in the cookie jar. "Eyes open. I want to look into yours when you come."

This moment is so intimate and passionate. I don't think I've ever had anybody make love to me like Barron is right now. We just met hours ago—we should be fucking like rabid dogs—and yet this differs from anything I've ever experienced.

With his eyes on mine, his hand cradling my neck, he moves in and out of me, completely focused on my pleasure. He smiles and leans forward to give me a gentle kiss. "Let go and come for me."

Just like that, I do, my orgasm his to command as I silently crest over, my pussy pulsating as I lock my ankles around the small of his back.

Barron groans. His jaw clenched as my cunt pulsates and milks him for his seed.

I flash my big brown eyes at him. "Did you come?"

"No, bunny."

"Why not?" I gasp, still trying to catch my breath.

His voice is gravelly, as if this is taking everything out of him. "Because I'm not done with you yet."

"Oh." I stare up at him with wide eyes.

"Yeah," he grins. "Oh."

Barron lets my leg down and rolls to my side, pulling me with him. Within seconds, I'm straddling him, his cock still fully seated inside my body.

"Impressive." I smile down at him and roll my hips.

"Mmmhmmm. Ride me, Betty. Nice and slow. Then I'll fuck you hard like you want."

I sit up straight, any self consciousness I normally have about my belly or large breasts nonexistent in front of this man. The way he looks at me—it's like I'm the most beautiful, sensual, exotic woman he's ever seen.

He doesn't have to say the words—I feel beautiful in front of him by the way he looks at me.

Rolling my hips and riding him slowly, I focus on his pleasure as he slides his big hands up my thighs and over my sides to cup my breasts. "I like this. Do I feel good?"

"You feel amazing." His husky voice and soft words caress my mind, while his strong hands caress my body. "What do you like about it?"

"It's slow and unhurried. I don't know. I feel connected to you right now."

"Have you ever been in love, Betty?"

His question takes me by surprise. "Honestly? No."

"Then you've never made love." He says with an air of authority.

I suppose he's right. Nobody has ever cared about me as much as I did them. I've had boyfriends, but none of them were guys I saw forever with.

"Have you?"

He brings his gaze up from my breast to meet my eyes, his head performing a slow shake. "I thought I was once, a long time ago, but honestly, I don't think I've ever been really in love."

I lick my lips. "Tell me what happened?"

"Get under the covers with me." As soon as he says that, I realize there's a chill in the air and we're both completely naked besides our socks and the sweatpants bunched around his ankles.

I climb off of him and he rolls to the other side of the bed, pulling down the blankets and patting the soft cotton fitted sheet with his big hand. "Lie down, bunny."

Why on earth do I like him calling me that? It's a silly little pet name, and yet I know it's mine and only mine. Something about it rolling off his tongue makes me feel cherished, and I believe he'd do anything for me as long as I was under his protection.

As long as I was his.

Dear God, I want to be his.

I crawl into the bed next to him and he pulls me into his chest, wrapping his arms around me after pulling the blankets on top of us. Cocooned in warmth, his body temperature heats my skin as he runs his hands up and down my back, brushing my ass with every swipe. He caresses me, but also with enough sensuality to remind me where we are and who we are to each other.

Lovers.

"You were saying?"

He brushes the hair from my face and strokes my cheek with his forefinger. "I was married many years ago when I was in the military. We started off as high school friends and reconnected at our ten-year reunion. After that we chatted online a lot, especially when I was deployed. She felt stuck in Branson and idolized my globe-trotting lifestyle, and I don't know—I guess I felt like I could save her by giving her a way out of there. We tried for a good six years to make it work. While we enjoyed each other's company, we never really had any passion for each other. Once I made E-9 and had to move again for another assignment, she told me she wanted to go back home to Branson and asked for a divorce."

"You don't sound angry."

"I'm not." He shakes his head and smiles softly. "She's happy now, and that's all I ever wanted for her."

"That's very mature of you." I bite the inside of my cheek, thinking about the best way to phrase this. "I don't think—actually, I know I've never dated someone like you before."

I hope he doesn't get freaked out because I use the word *dating*. Guys are so sensitive about women latching on to them too quickly.

He flashes me a knowing smile. "Because before me, you only *dated* boys. I know, because when I was your age, I was a boy. Young men don't understand or appreciate intimacy. They're only focused on getting off."

"Do you not want to get off?" I slide my hand under the smooth sheets, skimming the front of his thighs but not actually touching the goods.

And damn, they are good.

He draws in a slow breath, his eyes sparkling as he grips my hand and wraps my fingers over his still hard cock, sliding up and down lazily, but with enough pressure that I'm definitely jerking him off.

Or on—as the case may be.

"Of course I want to get off and I will be fucking you tonight—many times, many ways, and on every surface of this million-dollar vacation home—but I enjoy intimacy too. Since we fell into bed quickly, I want to be sure you don't think I'm only looking for a mindless fuck. I'd like us to enjoy ourselves by exploring everything each other offers—tonight and beyond."

Licking my lips, I move forward and press my nose to his. "It's a date."

He kisses me gently, letting go of my hand and sliding his fingers into my hair to deepen the kiss. "Are you ready to be fucked?"

"Yes."

"Are you ready to come again?"

I bite my lip. "I honestly don't know if I can again."

"You can, bunny. I'm going to get you there and keep you there all night."

He's making promises to my mind and body—and I believe every word.

I think I've graduated from the bunny hill to the double black diamond.

VETERAN
K9
TEAM

REPORTING
FOR DUTY

Chapter Seven
Barron

It's been a long time since I've made love to a woman for hours. Even though I've come multiple times and she's climaxed a cool dozen, I can't keep my hands off her.

It's after midnight and we're raiding the refrigerator looking for food while Sarge watches from her bed, always ready for a snack.

Walking around this big house in a bathrobe, I'm fantasizing about what life will be like when we get back to Spring City. Betty lives in an apartment but hopes to buy a house in the spring. I'm thinking if things go well, she'll move in with me instead, but I'm not going to tell her that.

Not yet, anyway.

I come on strong in most situations—it's the retired Sergeant Major in me—but not typically with women. With women, I take the laid back approach, letting them come to me—although not many have over the years.

Betty is different though and I know with every fiber of my being she's the one for me.

Holy shit. Just like Linc said.

So strong are my convictions that I no longer give a fuck that I'm old enough to be her father.

It makes me wonder though. "Betty?"

"Yeah, babe?" She flashes me a smile from the kitchen island, where she's attempting to assemble dinner with the handful of snacks they have in the house. I guess they were planning on eating out every night, but that plan was shot to shit when the blizzard rolled in.

"Where's your dad?"

Her smile falls. "What?"

"You're having this girls getaway with your mom. The two of you are obviously very close, but you haven't mentioned a dad yet."

"That's because there isn't one."

"Tell me about it?" I repeat her words from earlier.

Betty shrugs and returns to the meat and cheese plate she's building for us. "There's not a lot to tell. He knocked up my mom in high school and moved her to Arizona—away from their hometown in northern Utah. Within a few weeks of being born, he skipped out on her, me, and everything else."

"Fucking bastard," I mutter under my breath.

She giggles, hearing me loud and clear. "Yeah, he is. I looked him up when I was in high school. He moved back to their shit town in northern Utah and ended up impregnating some other girl. This time, he stayed and married her. We joke that her father must've owned a lot more guns than my grandfather."

"No stepdads?"

"Nope. My mom didn't date while I was growing up. Honestly, it's one reason I moved to Spring City. I'm hoping the distance will give her the freedom to find someone who will make her happy."

"She hasn't dated at all? In twenty-three years?" I scoff at the idea. No dating—does that also mean no sex? Is she completely tethered to and dependent upon Betty? And if so, how much is she going to hate me?

Betty walks over with the meat, cheese, and cracker plate, setting it on the table and sitting in my lap. "My father left us with nothing and she had to bust her ass for everything we had. She wasn't going to risk somebody coming in and taking it from us, so she never seriously dated, but she had a couple friends with benefits over the years."

"Do you know that for a fact?" I can't imagine having those conversations with my mom or dad when I was a teenager. We did not discuss those topics in my home, but as a boy, it wasn't a big deal for me. I'm sure my sister would've liked to have that type of open dialogue, but maybe not.

"My mom and I talk about everything. Because she was a teenage mom, she was very open with me about sexuality. She wanted to make sure I did not become a teenage mom myself. I was on birth control starting at sixteen and educated in condoms and menstrual cycles and all of that stuff long before my peers. My mom didn't want me to be afraid of sex like she was as a kid, or think it was this forbidden thing I had to sneak around and do —like her."

"Your mom sounds pretty amazing. She's going to hate me, isn't she?"

"Not when she sees how happy I am with you." Betty shakes her head, feeding me a cheese and sausage cracker sandwich.

Chewing absentmindedly, I slide my hand in between her thighs as she noshes on her own bite.

Without speaking a word, Betty parts her legs and grants me access. I fucking love how in tune our bodies are to each other and how she wants me as badly as I want her.

I slide the tip of my forefinger over her clit, her body jerking with the simple touch. "Are you sore?"

"Yes."

"Do you want me to stop?"

"No."

"Good girl." Grinning, I kiss her neck and slide my hand up to cup her breast. We're both wearing bathrobes supplied by the house, so it takes nothing for me to peel open the sides and expose her puckered nipple.

"Mmmm," I growl low in my throat, lowering my head and sucking it into my mouth.

Betty forgoes the plate of food and slides her hand into my hair, holding me against her breast. "Why does this feel so good every time?"

"Because your body was made to be my playground."

I murmur against her skin, sucking and biting, moving from one breast to the other and back again.

"I guess you're not hungry." She hums as I lavish attention on her.

"I'm hungry—for you." Once again, my hand finds its way between her legs, where her pussy is wet and ready for me. "Which rooms have we had sex in already?"

At some point we decided that this was the game we will play this evening—christen every room in the house, besides her mothers.

She giggles. "Bedroom, bathroom, and living room, if you count what we did on the floor in front of the fireplace."

"Did you come?"

"Yes."

"Then it counts." I slide two fingers inside, her cunt dripping wet. "My bunny wants to be fucked, don't you?"

"Yes," she says in a whisper.

"Stand up and bend over the arm of the couch." I pull my fingers out of her and help her to her feet, following her with my hands on her hips.

Betty immediately bends over with her feet shoulder width apart, arching her back and looking over her shoulder at me with a coy smile on her lips.

I flip the end of the robe up over her waist to expose her perfectly round ass, pussy lips glistening in the dim overhead lights. I can't stop myself and drop to a squat, plunging my tongue deep into her weeping hole.

"Ahhh," she cries out.

"Dessert," I growl, but I doubt she can understand me with my mouth full.

Just when I think she's close, I stand up, grab hold of my dick, line up, and thrust my hips forward—sinking balls deep into her glorious body. She's hot and wet and fits me like a tailor-made suit.

Perfect.

I take her hard and fast this time, pumping my hips and chasing my release, which doesn't take much. As soon as her body shakes, her cunt clamping down on me and milking me for every drop I have, I explode and fill her with my seed.

"Goddamn." I roar, my fingers digging into her hips as I come hard again. I can't believe I even have anything left inside of me and yet, if she turns around and says she wants more, I'm damn well going to give it to her.

Betty slumps forward on the couch, panting. "No more. I can't take it anymore."

I chuckle, slowly pulling back so that my cum drips out and trickles down her thigh. "Shower and bed?"

"Quick shower and no funny business." She opens her eyes slowly and looks at me, a half-smile on her face.

I raise my hands. "The last time we were in the shower, you're the one who attacked me."

She rolls her eyes. "I didn't attack you. I dropped the soap and when I bent down to pick it up, your cock was in my face. What else was I supposed to do but swallow him whole?"

"Well, then I suggest you don't drop the soap this time."

"I make no promises. It's very slippery." Betty grabs the meat and cheese plate, popping two stacks in my mouth and then turning, popping a couple in her mouth before setting the plate near the sink. "Will you turn off the fire while I run upstairs?"

"No problem." I grab us a couple of waters and turn off the fireplace before looking out the giant bay window overlooking the ski resort.

"The snow has finally stopped falling," I say to no one. Knowing Colorado, it's going to be a beautiful clear sunny blue sky day tomorrow. The fresh powder will have people clamoring to get up top and ski their happy butts down the plush trails. Hell, we might be some of the first people on the slopes tomorrow. That is, we would be, but given the choice between skiing fresh powder and snuggling in bed with Betty, I'm picking Betty.

We heard from Linc and Brandi a couple hours after they got settled in the Ranger station, but that was a good eight hours ago and I haven't heard from him since. I know if he was in trouble, he would radio. Frankly, we've been too busy to give them much thought.

I wonder if he's treating my future mother-in-law well, or is he being a dirty dog like I know he can be?

Fuck. Part of me wants to call him and tell him to keep his shit in his pants, but at this point, it's probably too late.

If anything could happen between them, it's already happened.

Double fuck.

I climbed the stairs to find Betty brushing her teeth, her eyes wary.

"You really are tired, aren't you?"

She nods, spitting out the toothpaste and rinsing her mouth. "I have hit a wall and I'm exhausted."

I offer her my hand. "Come on. Time for bed."

I tuck her in, kissing her lips gently. "I'm going to clean up and then I'll slip into bed beside you. Can you sleep while I hold you?"

She snuggles with a pillow and scoots her butt towards the middle of the mattress. "I'll be waiting right here for you."

"Good girl."

Returning downstairs, I find Sarge waiting for me at the base of the stairs. She's been super patient with us today, letting me pleasure Betty whenever and however I want without cock-blocking me. A total one-eighty from how she acted as a puppy.

Sarge, as an eighteen-month-old puppy, was the number one cock-blocker in my unit. She was possessive of all of us, but especially me, and if a woman came around, she'd find a way to be the center of attention.

I grab her bed and raise my eyebrow. "Can you carry your old body up the stairs one more time, or do you need me to carry you?"

She's already climbed them twice today, which is two more times than I think she would've preferred. She sighs —or whatever a dog does that seems like a sigh—and sits down on her haunches as her answer.

"Crap. I guess I'm carrying you."

I get her settled in the bedroom in front of the fire, which we have set to low. I love my girl. She's been the only constant in my life for the last twelve years, but I know her days are numbered. If I'm lucky, I'll get another year or two with her, but sometimes I worry it's only going to be months. The stress of wondering what I'm going to do once she's gone has weighed on me for a while. In actuality, today is the first day the idea has not consumed me, my future looking bright now that I've met Betty.

Love is a crazy thing.

I know I'm in love by the gut-churning turmoil settling in my stomach. Too far gone to protect my heart, I now have to play this out and see where we end up. It's going to hurt one way or another, so all I can do is give her my love and affection—not through words, but through actions. If it's what she's looking for, it'll all work out.

I have to believe that.

Sarge lies down in her bed and I sit beside her for a second, stroking her fur. I can hear Betty's breathing, slow and even, which leaves me to believe that she's fast asleep.

Quietly, I whisper to my dog—my confidante, my best friend. "What do you think, Sarge? Can she come home with us? Can she live with us? Do you think she's the one?"

Sarge nuzzles my hand and then licks my fingers as if to say yes.

"I think so, too."

After washing my face and brushing my teeth, I crawl into bed next to Betty, sliding my arm around her waist and pulling her back against my chest. Everything about her at this moment feels right. My spirit is so settled, I fall instantly to sleep.

VETERAN
K9
TEAM

REPORTING
FOR DUTY

Chapter Eight
Betty

Waking up with a smile on my face, I slide my hand over the thick arm draped over my waist. Barron's breath blows gently against my neck and shoulder. I wiggle my ass the slightest bit and he stirs, his hand sliding over my belly and in between my legs.

"Good morning, bunny."

"Mmmm. It certainly feels like a good morning. What do you say to coffee and hot tub to start the day?"

He lazily circles my clit with his middle finger and doesn't answer. It takes everything within me not to arch into his touch, instead wanting him focused on the task at hand. "Babe?"

"What?" he grumbles at me.

"Coffee and hot tub?"

"I was thinking you could ride my cock this morning instead."

I roll onto my back to find him looking at me with one eye open, a lazy half smile on his face.

"How about a compromise?"

"I'm listening."

"Meet me in the hot tub with two mugs of coffee and I'll ride your cock in there."

His hand magically withdraws from between my legs. "You have a deal."

"I thought I might. I'm going to use the bathroom and then I'll meet you downstairs, okay?"

He nods. "Understood. I'm going to take Sarge out, so take your time."

By the time I get downstairs, Barron has coffee brewed and the jets are going in the hot tub. "Wow, it really is a good morning."

The sun shining outside of the hot tub windows is bright, and I wonder where my mom is. "Have you heard from Linc this morning?"

"Yeah, I talked to him ten minutes ago. He has to dig the snowmobile out, or somebody else is going to have to retrieve them."

"How long will that take?" I glance purposefully at the hot tub and waggle my brows.

He grins and slides me a cup of coffee. "Probably an hour, maybe two."

"Oh goody. We have time." I drop my robe, grab my coffee, and walk over to the hot tub.

Barron follows, taking a sip of coffee and offering me his hand to help me descend into the bubbles. Oh my God, the water is pure heaven.

"Speaking of time," he takes another sip of his coffee and sits it down before lowering himself into the water with me. "I have lessons in a couple hours and then normally Linc and I head toward Spring City around four for work tomorrow."

"We're here for another two days," I say.

He pulls me onto his lap and I throw my arms around his neck.

"How do you want to play this? Do you want me gone before your mother gets here, or am I staying until I leave to teach lessons? Or do you want to meet me at the lodge after the lessons and introduce me and Brandi there?" Barron chuckles. "I have to admit—this is the first time I'm meeting somebody's mother who is my age."

"Are you nervous?"

"Of course, I'm nervous. What if she hates me?"

"She's not going to hate you." I roll my eyes. "Although, I'm sure she'll be shocked that I spent our time apart by bringing a big sexy stranger home to fuck his brains out. That's not my normal go-to vacation activity."

Sliding my hand under the water, I find my man hard for me again. He scoots forward and I wrap my legs around him, sinking down on his cock. My eyes flutter close as I smile, a soft sigh escaping my lips. "This is such a good way to get going in the morning."

Barron sucks in his breath while his hands slide up my back to massage and cradle my neck. "So, bunny? What do you want to do?"

I have to admit, making love in a hot tub is not nearly as easy as one would think. There's no surface to gain stability or traction with—the seats are smooth and curved for comfort, not sex—and the water provides a buffer to decent motion. Plus, I think it's taking away some of my lubrication.

Still, sitting here with my arms wrapped around my man, impaled on his cock, enveloped in hot, bubbly water —it's pure heaven.

"I think the least awkward option is to meet you at the lodge after your lessons, but before you head back to the Springs."

"I think so too. Can we have dinner this week?"

"Of course." I lean forward and kiss him, putting all of my feelings into the one simple act. How is it possible that I am completely crazy about this man in twenty-four hours?

Shit, less than twenty-four hours and yet I can't imagine my life without him.

We continue to make love—slow and casual—neither one of us really intent on climaxing, but instead, enjoying the feel of each other.

Sarge makes a small woof sound at the same time we hear—"Oh my God!"—my mother's voice pitching in shock from the living room.

Barron's arms wrap around me tight, pulling me into his chest and shielding me from view.

I glance over his shoulder at my mom and a man— Linc. "Mom?"

"I'm so sorry." She turns away, the other man's back already to us.

Barron's voice is deep and growly. "Linc?"

"Yeah." He chuckles.

"Your back better be turned."

More chuckling. "It is."

I hiss in Barron's ear. "I left my robe in the kitchen."

"Take mine and then bring me yours, unless you want me greeting your mother with a fucking hard on," he hisses back.

"Mom, can you give us a few minutes?"

"Yes, sweetheart. Of course. I'm so sorry."

"Wait. Why is your knee wrapped up?" There is a giant wad of ace bandages covering her left knee.

"That's a story for when you and your friend are dressed. I'm going to go upstairs and take a shower." She moves toward the stairs.

Linc, with his back to me, stuffs his hands in his pockets and shrugs. "I guess I'll head back to the lodge and check-in with dispatch. See you soon."

"I'll walk you out," my mom says.

As soon as they're outside, Barron tilts his head back and groans, "Fuck."

"Well, that was... new."

"Just kill me now," he grumbles.

I playfully put my hands around his throat and jostle his body. "It's fine. Although, now that my mom has a brace on her knee, I don't know if we're going to make it to the lodge this afternoon."

He wraps his hands around my waist and lifts me off of him, kissing my lips. "Let me go get your robe."

He's out of the tub and has his robe wrapped around him before I can turn around. Seconds later, he's handing me my robe and lifting me out of the tub. "I'm going to get dressed and take off. We'll save the meet-and-greet with your mom for later today or later this week?"

"That's probably a good idea."

Barron leans down and pulls me against his body, kissing me deeply this time. His touch is full of unspoken words, letting me know that despite our embarrassing predicament, this is not over. Within minutes, he's dressed and has packed up the truck, placing Sarge in the backseat. He pulls his phone out of his pocket. "What's your phone number?"

I rattle off the ten digits starting with an Arizona area code and smile when my phone beeps from the kitchen counter.

"Don't disappear on me, Betty." He cups my cheek, his green eyes searching mine.

I step away and grab my phone, returning to him in a few long strides. "I'll do you one better, babe."

I respond to him with my address, and the approximate time we will be home on Tuesday.

He looks down at his phone and nods. "You're not that far from me."

"Good, that means it won't take you long to get to me."

"I miss you already. I'll be heartbroken if you don't call."

"And I will be heartbroken if you don't come find me."

"I'll be waiting on your doorstep Tuesday night. That's not too creepy, is it?"

"In this situation? Not at all."

Barron presses his lips together, a world of unspoken things growing between us.

I love you is on the tip of my tongue, but that's crazy. That's just good sex talking, right?

Not good, but phenomenal.

Nothing short of phenomenal would bring me to the verge of saying I love you to a man I met yesterday.

"Be careful out there and worse case, I'll see you Tuesday tonight." I press my palm to his chest, right over his heart. The few minutes without physical contact are already too much for me. How am I going to last two days?

"Seems like a lifetime." He cups my face, his thumb swiping over my cheek.

"It'll give you enough time to decide if you want to pursue this."

"What is this, exactly?"

I shake my head. "I'm not sure. Certainly, I feel something, but I can't describe it."

He lays his hand over mine and presses harder against his heart. "I feel it too."

That's a non-verbal I love you if I've ever heard one.

"Me too." I grin and push him toward the door. "Go."

Barron kisses his fingertips and flashes them at me. "See you soon, bunny."

As soon as he pulls out of the garage, I close the door and run up the stairs to my mom's bedroom. I crack open the door to find her sitting on the edge of her bed wrapped in a towel.

"What happened?"

She rolls her eyes. "I got lost and hit a snowdrift. My ski got stuck in the snow, while my body twisted in a circle and I guess I sprained my knee. It's just swollen and it'll be fine over time, but right now it hurts like the dickens."

"Do we need to go to the hospital? We can drive down today if we need to." I can't believe I'm willing to give up a million-dollar house for two nights, but since Barron is driving home in a few hours, I'm desperate to follow.

She brings her eyes up to mine. "Are you really going to pretend like I did not just walk in on you riding a man in the hot tub?"

I blush and bite my lip. "I figured we'd get to that, eventually."

"Who is he?"

"His name is Barron Theroux, and he was my ski instructor yesterday. He stayed with me when you didn't come home, and he's also Linc's Search & Rescue partner. They live in Spring City and train police dogs and other canines."

My mom nods her head slowly, but she doesn't say what I'm expecting her to say. I almost want her to, so I probe a little deeper into what I'm feeling right now. Plopping down next to her on the bed, I let out an exaggerated sigh. "Oh, Mom. I think I'm in love."

She continues to nod her head. "You've never been a quixotic person, so if you think you're in love, there's a good chance you are."

"What?" That is not at all what I expect her to say. I

expect her to give me the, '*Now Betty, let's not get over our heads*' speech she normally gives me any time I say something even slightly outlandish like being in love with a man I met yesterday.

She shrugs. "Who am I to say what love looks like? I thought I was in love with your dad when he whisked me away to Arizona, but I think that was the dream of getting away from my overzealous family. They say when love hits you, it's like a lightning bolt. Many people say when they met their person, they knew it within seconds of meeting them. Did you?"

I do this half-nod, half-shake roll of my head. "As soon as our eyes met, I knew I wanted him. There was something special there and I couldn't stop myself from teasing and flirting with him. He was completely on board, teasing me back."

"Well, if he lives in Spring City, why not pursue something? Honestly, sweetheart, what do you have to lose at this point?"

I smile. She's telling me everything I already planned on doing. "Tell me about your night."

She lets out a weary sigh. "That's another story for another time. I'm exhausted right now. I didn't get very good sleep last night, so I think I'm going to take eight-hundred milligrams of ibuprofen, elevate my leg, wrap my knee in ice, and go to sleep."

"Would you like some hot tea?"

"That would be lovely."

"Okay. You get yourself situated and I'll grab you an ice pack and a hot tea."

"Thank you, my daughter."

"You're welcome, my mother."

I walk down the stairs feeling even more conflicted than I was before I came up. Not only does she not object to the tawdry scene she walked in on, but she's pushing me to fall in love. I knew if she met Barron she would like him, but I wasn't sure she'd approve of a relationship with him. Of course, I didn't feel the need to tell him that because in the end it doesn't matter. I love my mother and I value her opinion, but I'm not going to miss out on the pleasure he wants to give my body.

But now this can be our entire world—with no impediments.

I think that's what he wants too.

I hope a couple days apart doesn't change his mind.

VETERAN
K9
TEAM

REPORTING
FOR DUTY

Chapter Nine
Barron

Betty came by herself to the lodge and we got to spend a whopping twenty minutes together on Sunday before Linc, Li-Lou, and Sarge were fogging up the windows in my truck. We texted all night, all day Monday, and all morning today. She invited me over to dinner to celebrate her mother's birthday tonight.

I'm fucking nervous.

So nervous that my hands are sweating.

Parking down the street from Betty's apartment complex—because my truck is too big for the tiny parking spaces in front—Sarge and I walk the half block worth of concrete with lumps in our throats.

Well, maybe Sarge is cool. Nothing rattles her cage.

But me? I'm a mess.

I grabbed flowers on my way here, as well as a bottle of wine, both of which make me feel like a cheesy ass as I walk up the communal walkway to the front door.

Betty meets me at the stairs wearing a flirty skirt that

begs to have my hands underneath it and a sweet smile on her face. "I've never seen you dressed up."

I glance down at my black sweater, dark blue jeans, and black boots. "You should see me in a suit."

"I bet you're breath-taking." She throws her arms around my neck, claiming my lips in the middle of the hallway for all to see. "I missed you."

My anxiety settles for a second, the desire to lift and press her back against the wall while she wraps her legs around my waist strong. With her skirt on, it would be so easy too. "I missed you, too. How was the rest of your time on the mountain?"

"Pretty boring without you. Since my mom messed up her knee, she wasn't skiing, so we lounged around the house, played board games, ordered takeout, and watched the bunnies ski up and down the slope."

"Not as much fun as orgasms?" I arch my brow to lighten the mood.

"Not nearly." She smiles so wide that it does something to my heart.

"I brought wine." Showing her the bottle, she nods and takes the flowers from me.

"These are beautiful."

Leaning forward, I put my mouth to her ear. "I know exactly what facial expressions you make when you come and yet, I don't know what flowers you like. I hope to rectify that over the coming months."

"Months? That's a lot of dates."

"Not nearly as many as I want."

She interlaces her fingers with mine and pulls me

behind her down the hallway to apartment #223. "Come on. Let's get these in water and get the introductions over with."

As soon as the door swings open, a woman who is damn near a carbon copy of Betty hobbles out of the kitchen, wiping her hands on a dish towel. Her face lights up with a beautiful smile and although her hair is considerably blonder than Betty's, she has the same rich brown eyes.

She walks forward and offers her hand. "Barron, I presume?"

"Brandi." We shake hands briefly. "Nice to meet you."

She chuckles, tilting her head back to look up at me. "Wow. You are a mountain of a man, aren't you?"

"Mom!" Betty chides from her position near the floor as she scratches Sarge behind the ears.

"What? I think he knows he's built like a bear." Brandi double downs, but her cheeks flush with embarrassment.

I chuckle and hand her the bottle of wine. "It's been mentioned a couple of times in my life."

"Oh, this is nice." She hobbles back to the small four-person table set for two.

"Happy birthday."

Her mouth drops. "Is this for me?"

"Yeah. Sorry, I don't really know anything about wine, so I let the clerk pick it out."

She picks the bottle up and really inspects the label, then she laughs. "Yeah, I don't know shit about wine either, except that it's delicious. I'm sure we will enjoy it."

"How's your knee?"

"Oh, it's fine." She waves away my concern. "I feel stupid complaining about it."

"Linc said it could have been a lot worse."

Betty's head snaps up. "Worse?"

Brandi's cheeks grow a darker shade of red. "Did he? What else did he say?"

Linc has been uncharacteristically tight-lipped since we got back from the mountain, except when he's telling everyone about walking in on me naked in a hot tub. The motherfucker has been sharing that story with the whole Veteran K9 Center. Although I had my suspicions—knowing Linc and his instant attraction to Brandi—I wasn't positive something happened between them until right now.

The look on her face says it all.

"He hasn't said much of anything in the last few days."

"Oh." She bites her lip and sets the bottle down. "I'll get us glasses and a corkscrew."

"See?" Betty slides her arms around my waist. "She likes you."

I wrap my arms around her and rest my chin on the top of her head. This feels right, the ache that has been burning in my chest since Sunday morning finally easing up. "Does she like me enough to see me in the morning?"

"Are you saying you want to spend the night?" Betty lifts her chin and smiles.

"Yes." I kiss her forehead, the tip of her nose, and then her lips. "Or you can spend the night with me. Either way, I want to wake up with you in my arms."

"Not to mention all the things you want to do to me throughout the night." She waggles her eyebrows.

"Yeah, that too."

I loosen my hold when I hear the bottle pop. I didn't realize Brandi took the wine into the kitchen with her. A gentleman would have opened the bottle himself.

"I hope you're hungry, Barron." Brandi walks out with two wine glasses, handing Betty and me a glass.

"Starved. It smells amazing."

"It's my favorite, chicken cacciatore, but I told her we should eat her favorite on her birthday." Betty grumbles.

"Well," Brandi walks out with two more glasses, setting one on the table.

Four glasses total, but only two plates—what the hell is going on?

"I should probably tell you now. I'm not eating dinner with you tonight."

"What?" Betty takes a step back at the same time Sarge growls low in her throat. My fur baby stands up, walks over to the door, sniffs, and then sits down patiently.

Holy shit.

I'm ninety-nine percent sure Linc is on the other side of that door. She only does that for members of my team —people she's been around her whole life.

"I have a date." Brandi lifts her glass and takes a drink like she didn't just drop a bomb on her daughter.

I say nothing, watching the exchange and waiting for the big reveal.

Not a moment too late, there's a gentle knock at the door.

Betty's head swings around. "A date? With who? You don't know anyone here."

"Well, neither did you before Saturday." Brandi points out and walks to the door, opening it to reveal Linc standing there with the same bouquet I brought, making me feel like even more of a cheesy ass.

"Hey, beautiful." He leans in and kisses her neck, a most intimate of exchanges. "Happy birthday."

"Oh... plot twist." Betty whispers and looks up at me with wide eyes.

"I thought you two talked about everything?" I say low so only she can hear me.

"We do," Brandi says, not only hearing what I said, but also busting me on it. "But, I wasn't sure I'd hear from Linc again, so I saw no reason to tell her about our—" She blushes.

"Need to keep warm," Linc finishes for her with a big smile on his face, his youthful bravado allowing his mouth to utter stupid, albeit truthful, things.

I roll my eyes and slap palms with him, but say nothing.

"Hey Betty." He offers her his hand, which she shakes tentatively.

"Hi again, Linc."

"I hope you don't mind, but I really want to take Brandi out for her birthday."

Betty's mouth opens and closes, but words seem to elude her. She finally shakes her head and squeaks, "No, it's fine. Where are you going?"

"Dinner and live music." He glances at Brandi and she nods. "I would've suggested dancing, but that is not possible given the circumstances."

"No, not today."

Linc grins. "Maybe next time."

Next time? Damn, Linc. Way to stake your claim and intentions early. Good man. I guess the nineteen year old horndog I knew so long ago did grow up. I'd like to think I had some influence on that, but who knows.

The four of us stand around for a good thirty seconds in awkward silence when I notice the fourth glass of wine sitting on the table. I grab it and hand it to Linc while making eye contact with Brandi. "I assume this is for him?"

"Oh, yes. Thank you."

He takes the glass. "A birthday toast?"

"Give it a crack, man." I can't wait to hear what he comes up with on the fly. The boy has a silver tongue—always has—which is why his tight-lipped routine over the last few days has been so surprising.

"To new beginnings and good times ahead of us. I hope this birthday brings you everything that you not only need, but deserve. Happy birthday, Brandi."

Damn. That was actually pretty good.

We take a drink and then Linc slides his hand possessively on her back. "We should get going."

"Okay. Let me put these in water and I'll be right

out." Brandi takes her flowers and then hands Betty the bouquet I brought before grabbing her hand and pulling her into the kitchen to leave us alone.

Linc and I exchange a look. I shake my head, narrow my eyes, and lower my voice. "You son of a bitch. Talking shit at work for two days about me and you didn't think to mention your love life?"

He chuckles. "Hey, if you had caught me in a jacuzzi getting ridden by a hot chick, then I would've expected you to talk about it at work." He lowers his voice even more and steps closer. "As it is, we planned to sneak into the house and shower together, but finding you two blew that bright idea all to hell."

I nod, conceding the point. "Okay, I guess we're even. Stop fucking talking about it at work and never call Betty a hot chick again."

"Roger." Linc tosses back the last of his wine and puts the glass down on the table. "By the way, I don't plan on bringing Brandi back here tonight."

"No shit." I toss him a look that makes him chuckle.

"And I'll call before bringing her home in the morning." He smirks. "To give you time to..."

"Stupid ass." I mutter.

He responds with a cheesy ass grin. "I see we brought the same flowers."

"Yeah, that's embarrassing." I slide my hand down my face.

"Well, at least they know what they're getting from us."

"Are we ready to go?" Brandi grabs her wallet and

sets a giant bouquet—both of our flowers combined—down on the table in a pretty purple vase.

"After you, beautiful." Linc turns around with his arm motioning to the door, only then seeing Sarge. He bends down and scratches behind her ears before ushering Brandi out the door.

"Have a nice night!" Betty yells at the door as it's closing and then looks at me. "Oh my god."

"Are you okay?"

"I mean, yeah. Of course. But oh my god!"

I chuckle. "Yeah."

"Did you know?" She narrows her eyes.

"No, of course not." I shake my head. "But I had my suspicions."

"Why?"

"Because I knew Linc was attracted to Brandi, and I know what kind of guy he is. So I figured if she was into it, something was bound to happen."

"Are you telling me he's a slut?" Betty casts wary eyes at the closed door.

I intertwine our fingers, bringing our joined hands to my lips. "No, I'm not saying that. I'm saying he's a man that when he sees what he likes, he goes for it."

"Hmmm?" Her eyes sparkle as she looks up at me, a playful tilt to her lips. "Sounds like somebody else I know."

I grin. "Yeah, we're cut from the same cloth that way."

"Well, now that we have the house to ourselves—"

Betty turns into me, walking her fingers up my chest "— whatever shall we do?"

Wrapping my hands around her waist, I slide them down her ass, cupping and pulling her against me. "I can think of a few things."

She lays her hands flat on my chest and looks up at me with big brown eyes. "I have something to tell you before we go any further."

"What is it, bunny?"

"The last few days have been torture. I don't understand how I can miss somebody I just met this much."

Nodding, I brush the hair back from her face and grab her chin, tilting her head up. "I feel the same way."

"What does that mean?"

"I think it means we're in love."

She takes a deep breath and exhales it slowly. "Those words have been burning my tongue ever since I woke up in your arms Sunday morning, but it seems crazy to say them out loud."

"Yeah, it's a little crazy, but I say we lean in and embrace it." I frame her face with my hands and tilt my head down. The tip of my nose touches hers, while our eyes lock. "I love you, Betty. I am in love with you and I won't apologize for it."

She melts into me. "I love you, too, with all my heart. And I don't care if the world thinks I'm crazy."

I kiss her with all the love and passion I feel in my chest and then swoop her up into my arms. "Now that we have that settled, where's your bedroom?"

VETERAN
K9
TEAM
REPORTING
FOR DUTY

Epilogue
Betty - Three months later

My phone buzzes with a text from Barron and my heart swells at the written word: Home. Even though we've slept in the same bed almost every night—except on the weekends he goes up to the mountains or the occasional night when he pulls overnight security at the center—we've only been officially living together as of last weekend when I moved all of my clothes and a few choice furnishings that I didn't want to leave behind for my mom.

She's moving to Colorado this week—Linc is actually in Arizona with her right now, helping her pack everything up so they can drive here together—and although Linc asked her to move in with him, she chose to take over my apartment for the next six months until the lease is up. After being self-sufficient for the last twenty-three years, she's struggling to trust him and their relationship with her whole heart. While they dated half of November and all of December—spending almost all of their time together— she went back to Arizona in January and they've been doing the long distance thing for the last two months.

I know Linc hates it. He's miserable—which breaks my heart—but I understand my mom's fears considering what my father did to her.

Regardless, Barron and I agreed early on that we would stay out of their relationship, just as they agreed they would stay out of ours. Of course, she's still my mom, so we just avoid double dates whenever possible and talk about our men like girlfriends do versus mother / daughter.

Even though she is slow-rolling cohabitation with Linc, I—on the other hand—couldn't wait to move in with Barron.

We have a team meeting at four thirty, and then I'm coming straight home. Why?

I have a surprise for you.

You do? What? Why?

You'll have to wait until you get home, bunny.

Careful, babe. If you spoil me too much early in our relationship, I'm going to expect it all of the time.

My boss, Sariah Morvick, walks into the office that I share with three other social media team members, and sits at the small conference table we have in the middle of the glass-enclosed space. We're presenting to her this afternoon, so I'm a bit surprised she's here right now considering our presentation is still two hours away.

"Hey Betty." She glances at my teammates' cubicles, all three of which are not at their desks. "I heard you moved in with your boyfriend this weekend."

My jaw goes slack. "You heard that?"

Why would my boss hear something like that?

She shrugs. "It's a small office. I guess that means you're happy in Spring City?"

I nod. "I am."

"Are you also happy here at Taylor & Morvick?"

Panic quickens my pulse and I glance around the room, wondering if I am being set up. "Am I about to be fired?"

"No, no, no. God no." Sariah's eyes go wide and she

vehemently shakes her head. Smacking her forehead, she chuckles softly. "You've been here six months and I wanted to see how you were liking it. This was supposed to be a casual, informal mid-year conversation—" she rolls her eyes "—but I guess I screwed it up."

I sag in relief and chuckle with her. "I really like it here. This team is great, and I think we're doing a good job."

"You're doing a great job, and between you and me, I'd like to mentor you. I see a lot of me in you, and I think you could go far here—if you want."

"I'd love that!" My smile takes over my face.

"Great. I'll send you a calendar invite and we'll get started." Sariah pushes up out of the chair and waves goodbye as she leaves the room.

I can't believe my life. The last six months have been a fairytale and whirlwind of good fortune. First, I land an amazing job and paid relocation to Colorado. Then, I not only meet Barron—the only man I've ever fallen head over heels in love with—but my mom also falls for a good guy who treats her like the queen she is. And then my mom secures a remote nursing position, which allows her to move to Colorado to be closer to me and Linc. And now... my boss wants to mentor me at work. I'm truly living the fantasy.

I text Barron and my mom the good news, both responding with absolutely loving support.

The next two hours feel like a week as my excitement about getting home and celebrating with my man takes over my thoughts. After my team and I present a flawless social media rollout plan for one of our bigger PR clients, I pack up my purse and rush out the door. Twenty minutes later, I pull into the garage to find Barron's truck not there. I guess I've beaten him home, except Sarge is there, which means he's done with work for the day. There are a dozen red roses in a beautiful vase on the kitchen counter with a plate of my favorite designer cookies and a sticky note that says, "I had to run to the grocery store, but I expect you to be wearing polar bear pajama pants when I get home. Love you."

Most men like lingerie, but Barron has a thing for the flannel pajama pants I wore the first night we were together. They have a Pavlovian effect on him, taking him from soft to rock hard in the matter of seconds—so of course, I had to buy them in every color I could find online.

I take a small bite of the confetti cake cookie—my personal favorite—and rush to the bedroom, shedding my clothes as I go. Piling my hair on top of my head, I jump into the shower and make quick work of rinsing off. Minutes later, I walk out of the bedroom to find Barron sitting on the edge of the bed in a sexy pose, his elbows resting on his splayed knees, his hands joined, and his dark green eyes fixed on me. Heat flares behind his irises and he subconsciously licks his lips as he catches me dashing out of the bathroom naked.

"You're home."

He caresses me with his gaze and pats the space to the right of him on the bed. "Sit down, bunny."

"Would you like me to put on some clothes first?" I giggle, practically skipping to sit down.

"It's not necessary for me, but if you want to..." Although his words give me the option, his actions speak differently as he takes my left hand in his and turns to face me. "You make me so happy, Betty, and fill my heart with the kind of love I didn't realize I was capable of feeling. Before I met you, I thought some people weren't meant to find their soul mates or live a life full of love, friendship, and passion. Unfortunately, for too many years, I'd been okay with that. Now I want to shake anyone who thinks that way and tell them to not give up, because if they aren't paying attention, the love of their life might walk right by. I'm thankful I woke up before it was too late."

Smiling, I try to pull my hand from his so I can wrap my arms around his neck, but he tightens his grip and drops to his knee in front of me. All the air is sucked out of the room as the realization of what is happening hits me like a wall of bricks. "Oh my god."

He smiles and pulls a ring from his pocket. "Things have moved fast between us, but I knew the night I fell asleep with you in my arms that I wanted forever. I don't need time to think or see how things go, because nothing will change how I feel about you. I want you—forever."

I can't stop the tears from rolling down my cheeks, my head bobbing up and down to say yes even though he hasn't said the words.

His smile grows wider, and my big bear of a man

blinks back the tears welling in his eyes. "Will you marry me, Betty?"

"Yes." I fling my naked body against his, and wrap my arms around his neck. "I love you so much and would be thrilled to be your wife."

Barron chuckles and settles me into his lap with his arms around me. He slips the ring on my finger, and I'm awed by how beautiful the simple solitaire is. "It's perfect."

He kisses my cheek and then my lips, cradling me against his body. "Like you."

VETERAN
K9
TEAM
REPORTING
FOR DUTY

Second Epilogue
Barron - Five Years Later

"I'm home, bunny. How are you feeling?" I call as I walk through the house toward the bedroom with a bag of cold and flu remedy. She's been puking for two days, fighting off chills and a fever since yesterday morning. I begged her to go to the ER, but she wants to try OTC medication today and promises we'll go tomorrow if she isn't feeling better.

I walk into the bedroom, disappointed to not find her in bed. God, I hope she's not throwing up again. If she is, our asses are going to the hospital as soon as I get her dressed.

Betty walks out of the bathroom, her face flushed and hair damp, her eyes wild and full of unshed tears.

"What's wrong?" I drop the bag of medication and pull her into my arms.

She rubs her face against my chest before looking up and resting her chin against my sternum. "I hope you really really love me, because if this is what the next three to seven months are going to be like, I'm going to be a miserable bitch."

"What?" I say before my mind can catch up with what she's said.

Three to seven months...

I pull back to look her in the eye. "Are you sure?"

She nods, tears streaking down her face as she reveals a white and blue thermometer length pee stick that clearly says *pregnant*.

"Holy shit." I hiss as my knees go weak and move to sit on the edge of the bed.

We decided early in our relationship that we'd let nature decide if we were meant to be parents. Not actively trying to get pregnant, but not actively avoiding it either, it's been five years and nothing. At some point I figured it wasn't in the cards for us, and even though I was a little disappointed, Betty is all I really need. After we lost Sarge a few years ago, we adopted a Shepherd and a Bernese Mountain dog, both of whom I have trained thoroughly. I thought our family was as big as it was going to get.

We get our kid fix by being aunt and uncle to Vale's kids—he's got a damn baby making factory going on at his house—and now Kemp's daughter.

"How do you feel?" Betty sits beside me.

"Overwhelmed. When did you start thinking you might be pregnant?" I stare blankly at the floor, a million non-linear thoughts running through my head.

We need to get to the doctor immediately.

Which room will we convert into a nursery?

What are we going to do about daycare?

Will Betty want to continue working? She's done so well growing her career. I'll support her either way.

"This morning. Actually, it was my mother who told me to take a test."

"Brandi knows?" My head snaps up, my gaze going to her.

Betty shakes her head. "Not yet, but she suspects. I wanted to tell you first."

I nod and say nothing, satisfied that I'm not the last to know.

Tears fall faster down her cheeks as she twists her hands in her lap. "Tell me you're happy, Barron."

The quiver in her voice is all I need to pull my head out of the fog. I pull her onto my lap and wrap my arms around her. "Bunny, I'm thrilled, but I'm also shocked. How far along are you?"

She shrugs. "Ever since I came off my birth control, my periods have been all over the place. It could be two weeks or eight."

"Holy shit." I mutter again. "We're going to be parents."

Betty giggles. "Pretty wild, huh?"

I squeeze her tighter. "You're having my baby."

"Yeah."

I press a firm kiss against her lips, trying to ground myself in the moment. Betty digs her fingers into my hair and opens her mouth, sliding her tongue between my lips, and instinct takes over. I roll her to her back and stretch out beside her, my hand sliding up underneath her shirt to glide along the soft skin of her stomach. Soon this flesh will be stretched tight, swollen with my child, and a flood of emotions pulse through every nerve ending.

Sitting up, I lift her shirt over her head and slide my hands appreciatively over her breasts before laying my cheek against her belly. "You asked me if I'm happy, but are you?"

"I think, like you, I'm a little overwhelmed. I only peed on the stick fifteen minutes ago. What if it's a false positive? I don't want to get too excited until we know for sure."

Exactly what I'm thinking. I don't want to tell her how excited I am if deep down this isn't what she wants—but damn, I'm more excited than I thought possible.

"If it's a false positive, and a baby is what you want, then I guess we'll have to start trying for real. I mean, practicing with you is no hardship."

Betty smiles and waggles her eyebrows. "Maybe we should practice right now? Just in case."

Chuckling, I pull her polar bear pajama bottoms off and spread her thighs, kissing my way up from her knee. "Like I always say, Bunny. You are absolutely perfect."

Coming next: Linc and Brandi in Mine to Adore

Second Epilogue

Most of my books take place in Spring City, Colorado and feature cameo appearances from characters in past / present / and sometimes future books from all of my series. Check out my website for a cross-over / series map.

Also by Kameron Claire

Want more **Witty** Tongues, **Wicked** Needs, & **Wild** Deeds?

<u>Hollywood Lights (Pre-Order)</u>

* Billionaire Romance *

Show Time (Securing Selyne)

Money Shot

Three Shot

Martini Shot

Long Shot

<u>Veteran K9 Team</u>

** Military Romance **

Mine to Cherish

Mine to Crave

Mine to Possess

Mine to Adore

Mine to Covet

Mine to Worship

Mine to Protect

Mine to Treasure

Hot Nights with the Boss

** Forbidden Office / Age-Gap Romances **

Dating the Boss

Flirting with the Boss

Teasing the Boss

Tempting the Boss

Rangers Football

** Sports Romance **

Play Action Fake

Quarterback Sneak

Personal Foul

Two-Point Conversion

Red Zone

Man to Man Coverage

Short Story Collections and Bundles

Animal Attraction 4-Story Collection

Vegas Nights 4-Story Collection

Last Stand Saloon 4-Story Collection

Instalove Bundle

Grayson Enterprises Series

Bedding the Boss

Enticing the Ex

Tempting the Teacher

Wedding the Widow

Exclusives and Sneak Peeks

Get exclusive stories, updates, sneak peeks, and special content only available to subscribers...

Join our Mailing List Today!

Sign Up Here

About the Author

 USA Today Bestselling Author Kameron Claire writes stories with witty tongues, wicked needs, and wild deeds. Her books emphasize strong female leads and the protective alpha males who know how to love and support kick-ass, take-charge women. Many of her books contain military veterans, boss babes, gentle but dominant men, and goofy K9 hijinks.

Find her everywhere via linktr.ee/kameronclaire
Signed Paperbacks and discounted eBook bundles are available exclusively on her store
Subscribe to the Witty, Wicked & Wild community and read all her books online for as little as $5 a month.